NICHOL GOLDSTEIN

NIXCOMIX
PUBLISHING

WHITE WITCH, DARK MOON

WHITE WITCH, DARK MOON
Published by NixComix Publishing

ISBN (print): 979-8-9870103-2-7
ISBN (e-book): 979-8-9870103-3-4
An application to register this book for cataloguing has been submitted to the Library of Congress.
First Edition: January 2023

Cover design by Fiona Jayde Media
Illustrations by Nichol Goldstein
Editing by Emily N. Keys / Lyric Editorial

PROLOGUE

elcome to my strange, odd, interesting new story. Have you ever heard of "Choose your own adventure" books? Well, this is that kind of story—but for grownups. At the end of every chapter, you will be presented with two options: do "this" or "that." Based on what you choose, the story will veer off, and new and exciting things will happen.

POTENTIAL TAGS: Graphic Violence, Major Character Death, Suicide, Murder, Explicit Sexual Content, Pregnancy

TAGS WILL CHANGE DEPENDING on your path. They may occur in your decision tree, they may not. Be ready for anything and everything.

After my last book, I'd promised someone that I would never kill any major characters again. I...I have broken that promise. I'm sorry. I have a problem. Buyer beware.

That being said, for those nervous about finding bad

endings, I've made decision-tree maps. In them, you'll find all of Reyanne and Zanthrand's paths. This allows you to focus on reaching both open and happy endings, should you so choose. This can be found in the end of the book.

It's assumed that you'll read this story more than once to explore the different possibilities. There are a total of 17 endings possible and it's up to you to find each of them. I wonder if you can…

LET'S GET STARTED!

CHAPTER 1

In a ruby red canyon littered with bodies, only two figures still stand on the battlefield. The campaign is over, both sides decimated, dragging out the forever-stalemate that refuses to let the land go. Neither side gains anything, neither side loses—though, tell that to the dead warriors that pile up in places like these. Their names are forgotten, bodies buried one on top of the other, their lives expendable and meaningless, wasted in zero-sum skirmishes.

Families have learned to give up hope the moment their heroes pass the threshold into the war machine, for no one ever returns. If they live, it's only to fight another day, not to plunge back into the open arms of someone who once adored them. Perhaps cradled them. Perhaps wedded or bedded them. It didn't matter. Once they were gone, they were gone.

This is a time of no hope, only outrage and revenge. It casts a haze of madness over the eyes of the wise, ensuring the way forward remains a simple, never-ending loop of kill-or-be-killed. There is no peace; there is no rational thought.

There is just "us" and "them," fingers pointing from every side.

Across piles of broken hands and feet and skulls, a cloud of metal-scented smoke hangs in the air as the only two creatures still alive circle each other with bared teeth. The sun is fading and the shadows grow long, yet they still see each other clearly, knowing one another far too well. Beyond faces and expressions, they've memorized each other's gaits and simple gestures. The lilt of every vocal tone. Even the patterned rise and fall of their lungs as they breathe.

Reyanne, the white witch of the Separatists, and her nemesis Zanthrand, dark wizard of the Dominion, have been far too in tune with one another since Reyanne performed the soul-binding spell years ago. She'd read many ancient texts describing the ritual, how to pray and bless and sanctify. It was supposed to draw his soul to her, allowing her to steal his darkness and convert him to the ways of the light… but she failed. From miles and miles away, she had wrought a different kind of bond, one she didn't mean to forge and now doesn't know how to break.

Dusk claims the sky as the white mage's staff ricochets sideways, her enemy's black magic penetrating her rune-ringed ward of protection as if it were nothing. He knew it was coming and knew exactly how to counter her spell, a clairvoyance his side of the war worships him for, and, sadly, a prescience for which the white mage is absolutely responsible. Knowing her folly, Reyanne glowers a frown that could not drag deeper if it tried. At least their connection goes both ways.

"I hate feeling you worming around in my head," Zanthrand growls, his voice a low baritone that oozes disgust. His haughty expression almost suits him, a scowl pulling at his dusky pink lips as his large, dark eyes lock on hers. His broad shoulders and large hands tell of his strength even as the rest of him is hidden beneath the black trappings of war. To witness him is to witness a God in its chiseled perfection, even if all you get is a glimpse before he closes your eyes forever.

His jaw is tight with anticipation as he stares Reyanne down, too close for comfort and ready to strike again. Her magical stores almost depleted, she is flagging, whereas he looks like he could continue for eons.

She knows better.

Through their unwanted connection, she can tell he's just as exhausted as she is, perhaps more so. He just hides it better. A tricky one, that Zanthrand.

"The feeling is mutual," Reyanne says, going for broke and pushing through one last spell from her arsenal. Raising her staff in an upward arc and spinning it hand over hand above her, she causes a whirlwind so strong it pushes him backwards, his feet sliding over stone. His arms cross defensively as he chants a counter spell, his full lips moving as Reyanne's enchanted wind takes on a dangerous edge, slicing instead of just repelling.

Long ebony hair whipping behind him, Zanthrand grits his teeth as the screaming gale tears swaths off his heavy garb, nicking and embedding knives of air into his skin before lashing a deep, painful slit down his pale face. With one last grunt of his dark magic, Reyanne's wind reverses on her in a bladed spike—one she dodges only just in time to avoid being run through, taking a slash to her side instead. Her mouth opens wide as she cries out. The inward curve between the jut of her hip and the line of her ribs lights on fire as her nerves howl.

Going to her knees, blood spatters in pitter-pats of red rain, seeping into the stained canyon floor and mixing with the blood of her allies. Her misting gaze lands on a fallen comrade beside her. His eyes show only white and his face is shaped wrong, concave in the wrong places.

She has failed him. Failed to turn the tide of the war, failed to seal the enemy away, failed to see beyond the dawn. Looking at the sea of dead behind her, she swoons, head swimming…until she feels a familiar tingle—like ice dragging over her scalp in long, wet, dripping lines.

Zanthrand's thoughts.

Amorphous shapes of sound whisper inside her, just as she knows her mind projects to him. She's not sure whether it's because of the invasion of privacy, the intimacy, or the disadvantage it presents, but their connection in this moment burns her throat with bile and floods her heart with rage.

He's worse off than she is. Sprawled, his hands press uncomfortably against the rubble of the battle-littered ground while he pants like a wounded dog. His nightshade wizard's robes are slashed open in wide triangles, showing the pallor of his skin and the crimson of his endless wounds. Rivulets of blood run down his face, forehead to jaw, flooding one eye and rendering it terrifying as it pins her down with its glistening—likely blind—stare.

He can't attack her like this. Finally, after years, she has him at a disadvantage. The best thing to do with a rabid beast is put it out of its misery, and now that he can't fight back…

Struggling to her feet, Reyanne groans as her wrappings of ivory cotton darken red with her pain. Her hair cascades, drawing like a tawny curtain over her green eyes and leaving her lithe body vulnerable as she stabs her staff at the ground, using the magical artifact to help pry herself from the cold stone. She is dangerously, perilously close to fainting…but so is he; she can feel it.

Suddenly, with a dark chuckle, the look on his face turns

to one of resignation. He's tired. Tired of this fight, tired of her, tired of their connection.

"If you're going to kill me," he says, "hurry up and do it. Otherwise, I will hunt you to the ends of the earth. This is nothing compared to what I'll do to you, white witch. I'll make it hurt. I don't mind. I know exactly how, and it has nothing to do with magic."

His glare burns, and she trembles. Not only from fear, and not only from her own pain, but from *his* pain too. That's part of it all—how their connection works—their emotions, thoughts, sensations are aligned, something they cannot seem to escape. She, too, needs this to be over. She needs to put her worst mistake to rest.

But…knowing his pain, feeling it as she does, she can't help but wonder: If she ends him now, what happens to her? Will she feel it? Will she live? Will she die?

What is she going to do?

Dear reader, the decision is yours.

If Reyanne chooses to fight, turn to page 9, (chapter 2)

If Reyanne chooses to escape, turn to page 98, (chapter 19)

Good luck to our main characters, and to you, dear reader. Let's see how this story ends. Beware, some of your choices may lead to short, unsatisfying conclusions. Others will take you on a journey that will make your heart soar… though it may also rip it in two. Some will titillate your senses; others will make you yearn for what comes next and leave you longing. The choices are up to you, and I pray you choose right.

If not, read again. And again. Find the happy endings you

so desperately seek. One exists regardless of which path you choose right here, right now. It's the *next* choices that will open the way to success or failure. It's the *next* choices that will save or doom you.

Make your choice, dear reader. Open the door to the future.

It's all up to you.

CHAPTER 2

Reyanne shakes her head, keeping her wits about her. What does her fate matter when the greater mission is at stake? Even if killing him wipes her from existence, the tides of the war will still turn in the Separatists' favor.

Zanthrand is the dark heart sustaining the Dominion, just as Reyanne bolsters the Separatists—all those who stand for righteousness. Her people would break themselves into halves if they knew their sacrifice would burn the Dominion's militant, oppressive regime to the ground. That sentiment resonates with her, the selflessness of it, for she would do the same.

Reyanne knows she is the spark that lights the flame. Should she die, she can rest assured that nothing incites a crowd like a martyr.

Zanthrand, however, has no such comfort. He would be seen as a failure in the eyes of his people. In the Dominion, if you died, it was because you deserved it. Because you were weak—just as he is right now, prostrated before her, bleeding, half-blind, and utterly spent.

If only she could have turned him to her side. That was all she'd wanted. They could have defeated the Dominion together. They could have done *so* many things. Instead…

He hears her thoughts and his eyebrows knit, expression softening as he stares up at his own fate. "If you have mercy like you claim, make it quick. Don't keep this moment alive, making me listen to you debate yourself. If I'm to die, let me die. But do it now."

She lifts her staff and slips off the ornate end, a hidden scabbard. Tossing the sheathe away, she releases a holy blade that glows gold with the power of her connection to the universe. It is a magic that will never drain or dim, always at the ready regardless of her exhaustion.

She approaches Zanthrand in faltering steps—quick, slow, quick-quick, slow. His lips press together but do not tremble. His clear eye remains steady as the other weeps blood. Lifting her weapon, Reyanne breathes deep, tensing like a coiled spring, preparing to ensure a clean cut.

He readies himself for a quick execution, dropping his head low and letting his black hair shift to either side as he exposes the thick nape of his neck. In her soul, Reyanne feels him give in completely. Her heart hammers and aches…but this feeling isn't his. She alone owns these emotions. Of the myriad of things Zanthrand feels, pity is not among them. Nor is fear.

Reyanne closes her eyes, listening to the eerie breeze caress the canyon's steep sides, and makes her choice.

Dear reader,

If Reyanne decides to kill her enemy, turn to page 12 (chapter 3)

If she can't bring herself to do it, turn to page 15 (chapter 4)

CHAPTER 3

*A*t her feet, fallen soldiers cry out soundlessly to Reyanne, branding her mind with echoes of their suffering. Their silent refrain crescendos, entwining with the sorrow of those lost in the distance, a mix of Separatists and Dominion warriors reduced to souls in the ether. White armor and black. How many more people will have to die for this war to end?

Just one, perhaps.

And it's not going to be her.

With a heavy hand, Reyanne slams a downward strike, her golden blade molten with heat. The cut is clean. Effective. And gut-wrenching.

The pain in Reyanne's side is nothing compared to the gouging of her mind as his thoughts rip away, tearing a scream from her throat as she cascades to the ground, draped over the headless body of her enemy. Moments pass while she convulses, dead, but not dead at the same time. Her head feels scoured, her thoughts singular once more, all of them crying out, *NO!*

Weeping, gasping, Reyanne presses a trigger on the long

line of her staff, now turned executioner's glaive, and an ethereal light beams into the sky. The dragon riders will see it and come for her…what's left of her, anyway. For now, she clings to Zanthrand's body, arms wrapping over his broad back. She may weep for him, she may mourn, she may even be grieving the piece of herself that was lost today, but that doesn't mean she did the wrong thing. Even now, she knows in her gut this was the best choice. The only choice.

Sitting back, she swipes the tears from her eyes as her body settles into a foreign normalcy, leaving her confident she can still lead this war to a close. Reyanne will cast spells that awe friend and foe alike if her Queen commands it.

Perhaps, even if she doesn't.

Reyanne's mouth curls into a vindictive smile. Oh, what damage she could do…

Without Zanthrand to balance her, to keep her clenching her fist around the moral high ground, her hidden darkness bubbles up within. His spells echo in her mind, their memories raging and raw, begging to be used—if not by her soulbound sorcerer, then by her. After all, if there's one thing she's learned, it's that the dark magics are powerful. It might be time to put them to good use.

Decision made, she knows that—orders or no—she will pull blood from earth, air, and sky. She will rain down destruction on the valleys of violence, ending all who stand, both black armor and white. Who cares what side the warriors fight on anymore? If they are willing to kill, they should be ready to die. And if there is no one left to fight, she will have finally brought the peace that has eluded the people for so long. Isn't that what really matters? If she wins, she wins.

Once the armies are decimated, she can turn her eyes on the Dominion itself. She can raze its black castle to the ground, turning its stone to rubble, its warmongers to ghosts, its blind sycophants to ashes and dust. The capital city may fall, its people may die, but who cares about them? After all, they were weak enough to let the Dominion rise in the first place.

It's their fault, she thinks. *The ends justify the means.*

At least, that's what she tells herself.

You, dear reader, have earned a <u>BAD ENDING</u>!

Remember, there are 17 possible endings, and this is just one. If you've found all nine Reyanne endings, start back at the beginning, and choose Zanthrand's path. Many diverging stories await you!

Good luck, dear reader!

CHAPTER 4

The sight of Zanthrand's head lowered in submission grips her, his fearlessness astounding.

He truly is the perfect adversary. His potential for conjuring is endless, his spells both learned from masters and devised all on his own, making his repertoire unmatched. His speed of thought in countering her attacks is formidable, and his ability to pivot through multiple strategies never fails to impress her. Reyanne has wished many times that he could be her teacher. If only she could have brought him to her side. Why couldn't she make the soul-binding spell work properly? Why did she have to fail?

Reyanne's chest heaves in endless breaths, and she drops her blade. He lifts his gaze to hers, his wounded face one of curiosity before a small quirk pulls his pained lips to one side.

"Not today, then?" he asks.

Everything in Reyanne's body makes her want to run. Run from his eyes, from the satisfied swell of his emotions in her breast.

"Perhaps you are too merciful, white witch."

Reyanne swallows hard, the bulk of her self-hate clogging her throat as she wonders why she's making this choice. He's wondering, too. She can feel it.

Spreading her feet apart, she wills herself to stay standing as she grasps the gaping wound on her side. With a simple press against a secret notch, her staff triggers, and she twirls her weapon skyward, calling the dragon riders to her with a shock of white light that shines into the heavens. A beacon.

But if her comrades see him, Zanthrand will surely die, and there's nothing she could do to stop it…

She can't let that happen.

Gritting her teeth, she calls off the beam and stares at him, that smirk on the corner of his lips pulling wider even as his face bleeds.

"Why?" he asks.

Reyanne doesn't know. If she did, surely he would, too. Is it weakness? Pity? The strength of her moral compass? Or is it the fact that Reyanne's whole life revolves around him? Who is she without him to fight against? To form her battle plans around? To usher from her head? To growl at?

To pine for…

Wiping that sentiment immediately from her mind, she knows she has to say something—*anything*—lest the thought creep in so he can hear it. But what could she possibly say?

DEAR READER, **how should Reyanne answer?**

If Reyanne claims righteousness, turn to page 17 (chapter 5)

If she decides to be vulnerable, turn to page 20 (chapter 6)

CHAPTER 5

"*I*'m not a killer."

"Oh, Reyanne," he grins as he bleeds. "You absolutely are."

She straightens, holding in a heavy choke of pain. "An enemy like you needs to be publicly executed! To set an *example!*"

"And you think that absolves you of sin?" he asks. "No matter who kills me, it would be you who led me to my fate. But this? Your delay only gives me a chance to recover. Escape. Overpower you." Stifling a small groan, he lifts onto one knee. "And I have no mercy, Reyanne. Escort me into your camp and I will kill your comrades, your generals, your leaders. And I'll finish you last. Let you watch everyone else die, all because you failed to destroy me now."

With a labored grunt, he rears up, thick droplets of red dappling the ground. Reyanne takes a step back, the air ominous despite his depleted stores of magic.

"Nothing is beneath me," he growls. "Showing me that I'm your weakness…? What a fool you are."

Reyanne grips her staff harder, leaning on it to stay upright. "I'm no fool. I am righteous. I will not kill a cowering dog, even if it tries to bite me for my kindness."

He takes slow steps; ones Reyanne is in no shape to flee from. Exhaustion threatens to take her balance, and part of her gives in to the feeling. Whatever happens, happens. She's too tired now.

Closing the gap between them, Zanthrand lashes out and grabs the back of her neck. She lurches forward to brace herself against his chest even as they both cry out in pain. One of his eyes is sealed shut. The other looks her face up and down while something like heat screams unexpectedly through his side of their bond.

"Maybe I won't kill you. Maybe I'll trap you in a window-less cage and keep you for myself. Maybe I'll make you mine in every way a man can." His voice drops to a murmur. "I admit my own weakness when it comes to you."

"Just try it," she says through gritted teeth. "I'll end you before you make your first move." Though it's all bravado. She feels like fainting dead in his arms.

He's trembling and his breath is coming too quickly. If they keep this up, they're both going to fall unconscious, and the Separatist riders will find them.

"Go ahead," he says. "Run. Fight me. I'll travel to the ends of the earth to get my hands on you." He leans too close, the scent of iron filling Reyanne's nostrils as his lips whisper over hers, grazing her skin in the barest of touches. "I'm obsessed. You'll never escape me…and you know it."

Her knees quake. His words have an edge, a blade she has no defense from. They fill her with…

. . .

DEAR READER, what is Reyanne's reaction?

If his words fill her with dread, turn to page 22 (chapter 7)

If they fill her with excitement, turn to page 70 (chapter 14)

CHAPTER 6

truth.

"I...I don't know who I am without you," Reyanne whispers.

Zanthrand's smile fades as he stares up from the ground. The sunset has turned into moonlight and his wounds look as black as his garb. His heavy eyebrows pull together as he hisses in a shuddering breath through his nose. Reyanne can feel him searching her feelings, so she buries her longing deep under her fear. Fear he knows. Fear he understands. She knows he sees it in his potential victims all the time. There's no need for him to see her as anything more than that.

"You are Reyanne of the White," he says, "child of none, born of magic itself. You are—"

"I am *nothing!*" she yells as he strikes her long held soft spot. "I come from nothing, live, eat and breathe nothing, and it's all I can feel other than the fury I throw at you!"

"Lies," he scolds.

Her wound throbs as she clutches it. The ache causes her

brain to center, focusing in on the sting as she mindlessly smears the grime of battle into it. If she's not careful—

"You'll get it infected," he warns, gritting his teeth through the pain as his irritation flares. "No stupid, insidious blood sickness is allowed to take you. Your life is mine."

She huffs out a hollow, empty laugh, trying to cover up her urge to cry. When his threats sound like that, it makes her fantasize that there could be something more between them—another thought she needs to snip right in half, so she lets the tears fall, cleaning straight tracks down her soot-covered cheeks.

"My life belongs to this war," she says, her voice on the verge of tripping over the lump in her throat. "Day in, day out, my only target is you. If I finally succeed in destroying you, I lose my purpose, and what else can I possibly be then? An overqualified mage to bring out at court to impress nobility? A magical monster to unleash, slaughtering thousands with a single spell? I can't do that! I can't *be* that!"

He doesn't move from his position, but the flats of his palms press into the dirt, his fingernails scraping little hand-fuls of rocks into his fists. He sneers at her. "What do you want from me?"

"I..." she starts, unsure.

Dear reader, does Reyanne want:
For Zanthrand to comfort her, turn to page 77 (chapter 15)

For him to leave her alone, turn to page 82 (chapter 16)

CHAPTER 7

Dread. Something coils in her belly, terror and horror and fear compounding their nuanced flavors in her veins. His gaze is intense as he grabs her nape harder, pulling her impossibly close.

"Did you ever stop to think I might like it more if you fight me?" he says.

Her stomach drops.

"Because I think I might…"

"REYANNE!" screams a voice from the sky. A familiar dragon blots out the moon as its rider searches for her, having seen her staff's beam of light before she disengaged it.

She tries to cry out for salvation, but her voice is gone. The touch of Zanthrand's lips against hers has stolen it away. He'd been regaining his power while her attention was diverted, taking his own magic from the heavens and stealing hers with their touch. Why didn't she sense this?

"I could spirit you away now," he purrs low in his throat as she struggles to push back. "But a woman so weak is useless to me. I prefer when you have your claws out."

With that, he releases her. His magic whispers with an all-too-familiar spell, and Zanthrand begins to mist around the edges, blurring into the scenery around him as he chants, fading into black smoke that will disappear perfectly in the darkness of the battlefield.

Reyanne shakes her head, rejecting the very idea of his sorcery, though she doesn't really know why. Because he's running away? Or just because he's leaving her behind?

She hates it every time.

"REYANNE!" she hears again as she falters, dropping to her knees while her enemy wisps away into nothing, escaping as he has many, many times.

She hates him. But she doesn't. The feeling is all-encompassing, then rejected completely. But no matter her conflict, that deep-seated fear of abandonment from so long ago remains. She was a child left behind before, and she is a woman left behind now.

Why doesn't anyone stay?

Unable to stop herself, she faints on the body-strewn ground.

* * *

"You have to kill him," Osric urges, having healed Reyanne's wounds in the castle apothecary. Magic certainly does wonders.

It took Osric hours to find her among the bodies on the ground, confusing her white armor with all the fallen soldiers littering the canyon floor. In the end, it was his dragon who sniffed out Reyanne's living heartbeat, cementing her eternal gratitude and loyalty to the stark white beast. With wings bearing crimson stripes like finger-smears of blood, Drago is the only dragon Njal Osric will ride, just as Drago will accept no other rider. They, too, have a bond.

Her voice just returning, Reyanne croaks, "I've tried. No matter how I come at him, he counters me."

"One must wonder how he can read you so well," muses Leif Cassian—the oldest wizard in the land—suspicious as he mixes a draught to help Reyanne sleep. His skills as a mage have declined, but as an potions master, he thrives. He still has a sixth sense about him, though, making Reyanne want to hide far away from his narrowed stare.

"Don't speak to her like that," Queen Annora scolds. "You of all people know how powerful Zanthrand is. If defeating him were easy, you would have done it long ago!"

Reyanne watches a familiar despondency fall over the siblings of the Separatist Leadership, as it does every time they speak of the newest Dark Moon. A menace at large, Zanthrand was born from the ashes of the original dictator of the Dominion, the formidable Seth Cassian—Leif and Queen Annora's estranged brother. Seth's death made them the last remaining two out of a set of triplets, which Leif said was both a relief and a tragedy. Reyanne has heard many stories of how the three were born and raised together, as close as siblings could be…until they weren't. Seth had been seduced by evil, killing the Queen's son and taking over the lands with his dark magic power, save for this one last Separatist stronghold, held precariously in the Queen's palm.

Zanthrand, Seth's dark apprentice, destroyed his master in order to claim power over the Dominion in recent years—and claim it, he did. He and his generals now rule their territories with more than an iron fist. It's one filled with needles, shards, and thorns.

"Please, don't argue," Reyanne says. "It gets us nowhere." Her skin flushes, and goosebumps rise suddenly, a familiar trickle of Zanthrand's awareness tingling her mind. She grimaces, waving her hand for Leif's sleeping potion. "I need to escape him. By any means possible."

Leif hands over the bottle, and it clinks against Reyanne's buckled armguard while the old mage clears his throat. "Then we need to plan an assault," he says. "All the mages behind you at once. With the might of our armies and the power of our magic coming at him from every angle—"

"Never!" Queen Annora balks. "Do you understand what a disadvantage you'll put us in? What happens if we lose? Our magical prowess will be reduced to nothing and they'll trample us. They may have superior technology, but aside from the Dark Moon, we have superior magic. It's all that's keeping this war at a stalemate."

"It's true," Osric agrees. "We're the ones drawing the wards around this side of the continent. Without us, the entire Separatist region falls."

"And we're the last thing standing in the way of the Dominion's success," Lilah Tai says, piping up from the corner while grinding medicines together. She always listens to their back-and-forth conversations with the patience of a saint.

Better stop their talk, white witch. You know I hear every word, Zanthrand speaks into her mind.

A terrible truth. That's why Reyanne doesn't allow herself to be in conversations like these. Having him in her head isolates her. Keeps her on the periphery of leadership and makes her seem aloof, a prominent soldier, but not a strategist. Zanthrand's presence within her is crippling, for no one can ever know about their bond. They'd kill her if they found out; of that, she's quite sure.

What lovely people you've committed yourself to, he whispers.

And your people are any better? If they knew of our connection, it wouldn't matter that you're the newest face in a line of tyrants.

You'd be overthrown by your own armies and anyone power hungry enough to reveal what a liability you are.

His grim emotion solidifies the absolute truth of the matter.

A faintness seeps in, signaling he's drifted off to sleep. Perhaps he's been *put* to sleep.

Good. At least now her mind is her own. She doesn't normally dive into his thoughts, but he seems to take great pleasure in scouring hers.

"I need to end him," she says, focusing back in on the conversation at hand. "We all do. But I agree with Queen Annora; we can't throw everything we have at this. It needs to be just me. He's prideful. He'll agree to a one-on-one duel if I provoke him."

Leif scoffs. "You'll never survive."

"There's no way we're letting you do that," Osric says. "We may not need to sacrifice all the mages, but perhaps we can just bring the strongest few. Myself. Jessika."

"And me," Leif says. "I may not be what I once was, but I can still fight. If someone is to lay down their life to stop the Dominion, I volunteer. I stopped the rise of the last dark Empire—"

"But only with our brother's help," Annora reminds him, bitterly.

Leif sighs, rubbing his hands over his eyes. "I didn't see Seth's darkness for what it was. This is my fault, beginning to end. Every bit of suffering is on my conscience."

Queen Annora considers. Her face falls into somberness and her voice comes out soft. "But you're the only family I have left. If you go, you'll never come back."

Another grim reality.

To that, Leif only nods. "But I'm ready. If fate wills it, it can take me." He tosses Reyanne a wide grin, almost familial.

"And if I can save the hope of the Separatists, it will be worth it to face down the Dominion, magic or no."

"I can't let you do that," Reyanne says. She clutches the bitter draught bottle in her hand, admiring the twinkles of azure as the candlelight flickers over its glass. "I won't let you die for me."

"For my kingdom," Leif corrects.

"No," Reyanne says. "We've lost too much already"

"That's what war is," Osric says, the back of his fingers slapping into his other open palm as if to drive his point home. "It's being willing to risk everything. It's honing your hate into a blade that can defeat your enemies."

"No. That's not right," Lilah states firmly. Everyone looks at her, surprised to hear such an agreeable person cut in this way. Taking a nervous breath, she sits up taller in her seat. "I would lay down my life a hundred times rather than see those Dominion scum survive, but it's not because I hate them. It's because I love all of you. I love our lands. I love our freedom. I fight with that in mind, knowing that, if my sacrifice saves what I care about most, then it was all well worth it."

Lilah's bravado puffs up her chest as she rises to her feet, hands clenched at her sides. "If you're going, I'm going, too. I'm good with a bow and arrow, and I can fight. This isn't your choice to make alone, Reyanne. If I choose to save what I love, then that's exactly what I'll do."

Osric pulls his full lips together into a thin line, running a hand through his tightly cropped curls. "Agreed."

Queen Annora takes a deep breath that fills her to the brim, holding it for what must be a painful amount of time before letting it out in a loud puff. "Then we need an ambush. If he's as prideful as you say, Reyanne, you need to deceive him. Lure him into a duel to the death. We'll take a small flock of dragon riders that will drop flame potions over him. Meanwhile, Osric, Lilah, Leif, and Jessika will portal over."

Osric huffs. "None of us knows how to do that."

"I do," Leif says. "And I can pull you all over with me."

Reyanne shakes her head, knitting her eyebrows in concern at his foolishness. "Your magic stores will be depleted before you even hit the battlefield."

"An easy target, then." Leif's smile is resigned. "I can be an added distraction. Perhaps buy us more time. Even one second could be all that's needed to change our fates."

Everything in Reyanne aches. Her wounds may be healed, but exhaustion takes over her limbs. Her chest is filled with little razors that cut every time she breathes. If they did this, so many wouldn't survive. Not only that, it's a disgusting, deceitful trick…though it may be the one thing that destroys Zanthrand once and for all.

There's no way to surprise her soul-bonded pair, not about something this big. If the Separatists go through with this plan, she'll have to make the case that they put her to sleep until the final date of the battle. But how can she do that without explaining why?

No. Even thinking it is preposterous. She needs to face Zanthrand alone. It's the right thing to do. The honorable thing.

Or maybe she needs to cut out the weakness he accused her of. For he is, indeed, a weakness.

Dear reader, does Reyanne:

Agree to let the Separatists help her? Turn to page 29 (chapter 8)

Decide to confront Zanthrand on her own? Turn to page 39 (chapter 9)

CHAPTER 8

"I'll make it happen," Reyanne says. "Get me a scroll."

It's only moments before her ask is shoved into her hands, her comrades brimming with nervous energy. Clenching her jaw, Reyanne shares in their tension. Even so, with a graceful flourish, she pulls her power from the air around her, drawing letters that spit fire as shimmering words emblazon themselves across the page, fading into ultra-black lines of deception.

There is no escape from this fight, Zanthrand. Not for you. Not for me. Meet me for a battle of wills, wits, and words in the Ethereum plain at the rise of the next full moon. Bring no one. Bring nothing. This isn't about the Separatists. It isn't about the Dominion. It's about my pride...and yours.

I have no weaknesses, no matter what you may think. Meet me and I'll prove it to you. The winner gets everlasting glory and the loser dies quickly. That will be the only mercy between us.

Live or die. It's time to see what destiny has in store.

I await your wrath, Dark Moon, as you now await mine.

Reyanne of the White

Each word is sickening. The strokes of her fingers make her a liar without honor. She wants to tear up the thick, manila surface and burn it. Perhaps vomit all over it. Instead, she clutches hard, marking crescent fingernail shapes in the paper.

She rolls it up, and Osric hands her a candle. The pale wax drips onto the scroll in a perfect, circular blot, and Reyanne presses her thumbprint into its scalding surface to seal the message, hiding her words from prying eyes. There is a shushing sound as she slides her palms over the roll and mutters "An'na kharoshi," making it glow a steady gold, just like the light of her weapon. This is now unmistakably from her, and Zanthrand will sense it even as the letter approaches his stronghold, never mind when he holds it in his hands.

A squawking sound echoes as a bird from the menagerie is brought into the room. Bright, intelligent eyes. It's not a carrier pigeon, but an eagle, and the difference in size and viciousness is not lost on her. Tucking her challenge away into a pouch on the bird's back, she pets it just once, not knowing if it will survive.

"Don't stop until you find him," Reyanne tells it. "Once you're close enough, he'll call to you, I'm sure."

Especially since he won't be able to communicate with me. Intimidate me. Search through me. I'll be a void in the universe until the final day, and he'll be beside himself with rage. Or fear.

Or worry...

Taking a deep breath, Reyanne looks at her distant compatriots, sadly the closest thing she has to friends. To a family. It's not good enough, but it's all she has.

"I need to be put to sleep," she says. "All day, every day, until the night of the battle."

Lilah's head cocks to one side, confusion taking over her face. "Why?"

The truth hangs heavy in Reyanne's heart, but her bond with Zanthrand is something she will never have the courage to speak about. Not to anyone. It's shameful, but also…sacred.

"I need to build up my stores of magic," she lies. "One wrong move, even just tiring out before he does, and all will be lost."

"But you need to eat," Osric says. "If you don't, you'll fade."

"There are ways," Leif says, looking Reyanne in the eyes for far too long.

She clears her throat. "I know a spell that will put me in stasis. My heart will beat, my lungs will breathe, but all else will remain still. I will not hunger. I will not thirst. I will just suck up the universal force around me until my cup is completely full. I know how to do this."

"Then do it," Queen Annora says. "Whatever you need."

* * *

Reyanne floats through dreams, ones Zanthrand claws to get into…and fails. But she gets glimpses of him. His face is furious and his magic pulses with ominous black power as he pulls at her mind. Any thoughts he captures are nonsensical, though, like an unraveled tapestry. You can follow a thread, but where does it go? The future? The past? Is it a memory? A wish?

Sometimes, in moments when his consciousness washes over her, it hurts her soul. A burning that suffocates her drifting mind. Other times, he's like the color blue; a cool and soothing balm. It's only when his intrusion is red, just like the aura of his weapon, that things get truly intense. His fingers touch her imaginary skin, leaving crimson marks of desire. She wants more, he wants more, but it will never happen. Especially not now.

Their bond has not loosened, but it is not the taut leash that normally chains them, either. It's more like silk. Sometimes you have it, other times it slips from your fingers.

There's not much time left. Reyanne's consciousness feels his panic. Is it for her? For himself? Either way, he's wasting his magic trying to get to her.

That can only be a good thing.

…Right?

* * *

The dried grass crunches beneath Reyanne's feet. She feels dizzy as the vestiges of sleep leave her. It's far past sunset, but the high moon lights up the night as if it were day. Zanthrand awaits as she stumbles forward, drunk on mind-befuddling elixirs that she can only pray wear off in time for her to defend. To attack.

A dark scar traces down her nemesis' face, his wounded eye now glowing a vicious yellow-gold.

"What have you done to yourself?" she asks, blinking heavily at him. She's completely vulnerable. If he came for her now, she'd be gone. Why isn't he coming for her?

Answering her thoughts, he *tsks*. "I said I'd prefer some fight in you, did I not?"

She wipes her eyes. "It will wear off soon."

"Yes, and then I suppose you'll show me what your trick is."

She doesn't even bother lying. Instead, she sways on her feet. Unexpectedly, he's around her in moments, keeping her from toppling over, scolding her between his teeth.

"How stupid do you think I am?" he hisses. "For you to go this far to hide something from me, it can only mean you've either found some true power I've not yet divined, you're bringing an army down on my head, or…"

"Or what?"

"Or you're trying your damnedest not to let me discover how deep your feelings for me go."

She tries to shove him away, her wits coming back slowly. "You'd like that, wouldn't you?"

He thrusts his large hand into her hair and keeps her close, the glow of his new eye dancing across her cheek. "What if I said yes?"

"You just want me weak." She tries to shake her head, but he holds her fast. She brought no weapons, and her brain has yet to grasp a spell.

"What if I said yes to that, too? But not your body, Reyanne. Fight me tooth and nail; I'll revel in it, I promise you. But soften your heart. Be weak for me like that."

Her head ticks slightly back and forth. "Why?"

"Because no one else ever has, and I'd like to know what it feels like before I die." His free hand traces up her shoulder, slow and tender. "Which should be soon, I'd imagine."

"As if you'd walk right into a trap." She tries to push him off, and fails.

"Think you're clever, do you? I know your dragon riders are coming. Even now, your mages are chanting their spells to invade our battleground, aren't they?"

Reyanne's eyes narrow.

"I have spies all over, my white witch. And one lives right in your infested nest. I believe her name is…Lilah?"

And now Reyanne goes pale. "Why would she—?"

"I have her sister. I've had her for years. We treat her well enough…so long as Lilah does her job. I don't need access to you to have access to your plots. I only need people beneath me willing to do my bidding."

Her strength increasing, Reyanne wrenches her body away. "Then why would you come here?!"

"Why? Perhaps I'm just curious to see how much of your army I can defeat before I fall. Perhaps I want to take out some key campaign members before I escape. Perhaps I poisoned your elixirs, so you'll be no match against me. Or maybe…just maybe…I'm tired of all of this."

The wind picks up his black tresses and toys with them, giving him an eerie beauty.

"And so, you'd give up your life?" she asks, disbelieving.

"Search my mind if you can, Reyanne. Or see if my potion will keep your magic—and our bond—on mute."

Her blood pounds in her ears. Closing her eyes, she breathes deep and tries to access her connection to the universe, to the chaos in the ether, to the beating of his heart…but she can't. "You really poisoned me?"

"Now, now. You can't be upset about a little betrayal. Especially since it's for your own good."

She sneers. "And how's that?"

He lashes out again, grabbing her by the wrist this time. His jaw is set and the tendons pulse at his temples as he grinds his teeth, staring her down. "I didn't know if you'd be stupid enough to try to save me at the last minute."

"Why would I—?"

"Weakness. And strength. But it would doom you, my darling. Everyone here would see us for exactly what we are."

"And what are we?"

"Soul-bound," he says quickly. Then, quieter, "Soulmates."

Reyanne's eyes fill with tears. No matter how much she fights it, she knows that he's right. All of a sudden, fear overtakes her. "You need to run. You need to run right now."

"Tell me I'm in your heart."

"You're in every part of me," she growls, trying to pull away, but he won't let her. Instead, he swoops in and takes her lips—a heavy, warm, open-mouthed kiss, silencing her.

Pulling back, he repeats, "Tell me."

"No!"

Still, he holds her tight, his eyes dropping to her lips once more. "Please," he begs.

"If I tell you, will you run?"

He shakes his head slightly. "I'm a lamb to the slaughter. A fool about to be ambushed. Remember how you promised me mercy?"

Her throat closes in on itself. She can't speak. She can barely see through the tears in her eyes.

"Then be merciful, Reyanne. Tell me you love me. Tell me we're star-crossed. Tell me that, if things were different, it would be just you and I fighting against the world."

"No," she whispers. He looks away in frustration until she caresses his face with the tips of her fingers, running them down the length of his new scar, the one she gave him, slashed from his eyebrow to his cheek. "If it were just you and I, we'd never have to fight anything in the first place. We could have peace. We could have a home. We could have…a family. Something the world never gave us."

His lips pull into a little smile then, a single tear falling onto her upturned face. "That would have been perfect."

At that, he shoves her back and unsheathes his blade just in time for a portal to rip open. Harsh, screeching roars fill the air as dragons swoop down from the cover of a thick cloud.

You can't save me now, Reyanne, he pushes into her mind. *Don't try. It's too late for that.*

Her heart wrenches. "Zan!"

"Shh," he tells her. *Remember. Our bond is our secret. Don't give the game away now. It's almost over.*

She tries to stand, but she's not fast enough. Osric and Jessika rip through the portal, with Leif at their side and Lilah close behind.

Lilah…

The traitor.

Think of the family we would have had, Reyanne. Think of the sons and daughters. Zanthrand steps back, eyes on the sky as leathery wings cover the pale glow of the moon. *Think of the laughter and the joy. Think of our bodies entwining and the love we could have shared. If you're to remember me, remember me like that.*

And then, he dives away from the portal, far from her. She wants her magic, but she still can't touch it. What has he done?

Looking toward the swirling vortex where the Separatists have intruded, Reyanne watches as Lilah pulls out a knife. The traitor drives it into Osric's side just as he begins an incantation, twisting it with a viciousness that hurts to witness. Jessika spins on her heel, but it's too late—Lilah has gone for her throat. Jessika had no chance.

Leif squares off with Lilah now, potions at the ready, but before he has a chance to use them, Lilah screams, "IS SHE SAFE?!"

"Yes," Zanthrand calls back. "And she's coming home to you." With that, he waves his hand and Lilah disappears to a place unknown.

The dragons spiral above, their riders waiting for Zanthrand to be far enough away from Reyanne to attack him with their deadly concoctions.

FIGHT THEM! she silently screams.

Instead, Zanthrand thrashes his weapon to the side, releasing and letting it fly far and away, landing close to where Reyanne panics. The blade's red beam sizzles the ground into cinders beside her as he moves further into the clearing, putting himself more at risk with each step.

He can't do this! Why is he doing this?!

Tell me you love me, he says into her mind once more.

I LOVE YOU! Now GO! ESCAPE!

But he doesn't. And it's too late.

The first volley of potions fall like hail from the sky. The glass shatters, the vile liquid inside igniting the dry grass with a low roar of flames. Zanthrand cries out in pain as they burn him, endless vials raining down from above, surrounding her darkest dream with an inferno of searing, flickering, blazing agony.

Mercy, Reyanne, he calls to her. *You promised mercy.*

And that, she did. With a sob on her lips and rage in her heart, she snatches his weapon and dives closer, the wards woven into her clothes weakening the fire into mere warmth against her. The blade sinks through his heart as she takes in the tragic sight of him—his ruined skin, his fire-wracked clothes, the tears sizzling on his cheeks.

His lips quirk up at the corners. "Th-that's it, princess," he whispers.

And then Zanthrand is no more.

Reyanne the White has finally destroyed the keystone of the Dominion's strength.

Reyanne the White is now the unequivocal hero of the Separatists.

Reyanne the White has turned the tide of the war.

And in doing so, Reyanne's heart has died, fading together with her soulmate. Her body may yet live, but she is already long, long gone.

As the joyous cries of the dragon riders fill the air, she does not laugh…or cry. Even as Leif runs to her side, she does not walk or talk or see. Instead, she lives only in her mind, dreaming of a home by the ocean surrounded by flowers. A place where she breathes in the cool, salt air while resting in the arms of a man with dark hair, dark eyes, and dark magic.

Reyanne has finally found the love she's always wanted, if only in a dream.

And there's no reason to ever wake up.

You, dear reader, have earned a <u>SAD ENDING</u>!

Remember, there are 17 possible endings, and this is just one. If you've found all nine Reyanne endings, start back at the beginning, and choose Zanthrand's path. Many diverging stories await you!

Good luck, dear reader!

CHAPTER 9

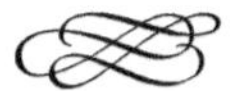

So what? It doesn't matter if he's a weakness or not. What matters is the moral high ground. How could the Separatists ever claim to be the voice of righteousness with such dirty tactics? Reyanne refuses to let her people sully their hands with such treachery. The Dominion will turn their underhandedness against them, and their allies may lose faith—especially when the backlash of the Dominion's wrath comes hammering down.

But if Reyanne faces Zanthrand alone, then it's no one's fault but his for being so arrogant as to enter into single combat, the Dominion's archaic philosophies in practice. The ancient texts declare: Despise the weakness of fear. Cut it out of you like a sickness, for only in strength will achieve your finest victory.

The Dark Moon's entire nation is built on power through conquest. Compliance through control. Peace, but only through mindless obedience. Asinine tenets Reyanne absolutely cannot abide by. It's barbaric. And that's why it must be stopped.

But only in the right way.

Ignoring the strategic conversation that still continues around her, Reyanne tosses back Leif's muddled concoction and immediately drifts off to sleep, a solid stone in her heart.

* * *

The air quality changes as Reyanne lies asleep in her bed, making her rouse and blink in a bleary-eyed fashion. She's been moved to her chambers—simple with no fanfare, but a nice, soft bed to sleep on, all feather down in colorful quilts and a gentle fire crackling in the background. Strangely, the room doesn't smell like warm ash or the comforting scent of embers. It smells like the air after it's been touched by fresh snow, though no chill tickles her skin.

It's the mirror gate.

Of course, it is.

Uncontrollable in its intermittent appearances, some-times the gate's visual opening closes the distance between Reyanne and Zanthrand. It's not a portal—though something like that happens, too—but instead, it's a window. One through which the soul-bound pair has tried to touch...even if only their fingertips...and even if only as an experiment. They felt tingles and shocks, but nothing more. The gate is so unlike the rips in the air which put them into each other's immediate physical spaces. At that point, all they do is attack one another until the universe tears them apart again.

Reyanne sees Zanthrand through the mirror gate, also lying down. His blankets are the furs of rare animals and he looks at her blandly, just as exhausted as she is. Seems they were both put to sleep by medicinal means this time around. It will keep the conversation docile.

To the death, then? he asks within her mind.

"I see no other way," she says, her voice rough as she tries to shake the cobwebs from her mind. Taking him in, she notices his injured eye is still seared shut, and fears it may never see again.

"It won't," he agrees with her unvoiced worry. "But I may have a way to fix it."

She catalogs his brain, something she rarely does, and sees the vague shape of a magic spell there. "That's a good one, if you can make it work."

"Oh, I very much intend to make it work. If I live that long." He breathes in deep, stifling a yawn. At times like this, he seems more human than murderous villain.

She toys with the fabric swaddled around her as she rolls to her side, facing him fully and trying to coax him into her plan. "If it's just the two of us, you have a chance. A fifty-fifty shot at winning."

"Or I could decline to indulge you in your little battle of wills and have a hundred percent chance at survival."

She sighs, rolling her eyes.

"Is having me in your head truly so terrible?" he asks. A silent question echoes, *Is having me in your* heart *truly so terrible?*

"Yes," she says to both questions. She means it, but she doesn't—that conflict rearing its ugly head again. "All I know is that I can't live a real life until the war is over. And the war can't end without one of us dead and gone."

"Willing to commit suicide, then?"

She snorts. "I have a fifty-fifty chance as well, you brute."

He smiles at her, sleepy as his raven hair spills over his pillow. He rolls ever so closer. "If you fight me, I'll kill you my white witch. I have no need for your self-righteous games. Not against my armies, not against my person, and not within my mind."

"I'm not playing games."

"Yes, you are. Your mouth spouts the Separatists' challenge but your heart aches with unbearable loneliness, driving me to distraction. Besides, you can't kill me. What would you be without me?"

She smirks, wry and sarcastic. "Perhaps without you in my head, I can finally take a lover."

A spit of anger flares on his side of the bond. "And that's all that's missing from your life? A man sheathed inside you?" His glare burns.

"A man in my arms," she corrects softly. "One who will tell me sweet, honest words. One who needs me." A lump fills her throat. "One who loves me."

His scar mars his stoic face. The moonlight of wherever he is casts him in blue, whereas she basks in the yellow glow from the pyre keeping her warm. She wonders if it's cold where he is.

Rolling away onto his back, he grasps his hands into fists, knuckles popping. Too many of his feelings are running through Reyanne at once; she can't make sense of it.

"I can't pick your thoughts apart," she says.

"Maybe they're for me, alone," he replies. "Did you have a man in mind, white witch?" It comes out with venom, as if Zanthrand would kill anyone she named.

"No." It's not a lie. "Right now, the only person in my life is you."

"How sad that must be."

"You act like I'm the only lonely one between us."

He casts a one-eyed glance in her direction. "The difference between you and I is that I know my needs will never be fulfilled."

"No one to sheathe yourself inside then?" she barbs him, her eyebrows up.

He surprises her by laughing a little. "Wouldn't you know? Wouldn't you feel it?"

Red-cheeked, she's tired of this conversation, yet the mirror gate remains open. She stuffs her face into her pillow out of sheer embarrassment, waiting for it to end.

"I'd hoped for more than a lover," he says quietly. "Someone to share a life with. Make a family with. Rule the world with." The last ends in a teasing lift of his brows.

She snorts. "Predictable."

"Is it?" he asks. "Everyone assumes I'd only bed a woman through violence. My people likely imagine me rutting into slaves, meaningless concubines, or the unwilling, keeping them under my heel."

She cringes. "Disgusting. They should have more faith in you."

He chuckles again. "Spoken by the woman who wants to end my life."

There is a long pause where she curls deeper into herself. "I don't want to."

"Apparently, it makes no difference." Silence settles in between them again, and his feelings dip into something that feels like despair. "For what it's worth…I don't want to kill you, either. And yet, it seems I must."

"Live or die," she agrees, tears welling.

He hums his agreement. Shuffling, he no doubt turns his back on her, as she has him—though she feels the tell-tale tingle against her skin, that special sensation the mirror gate creates when they try to touch. Zanthrand's so close, though he's also miles away.

"I'll make it quick," he promises, assuming the win and frustrating her to no end.

"And so will I."

* * *

Reyanne has long since slipped away from the Separatists' headquarters and traveled on foot toward Zanthrand's lair. She meets no soldiers on her path, no checkpoints. It would be odd if not for the fact that Zanthrand himself is helping her slip past his defenses. He looks through her eyes and knows exactly where she is, town for town, valley to valley. Anticipation and fear roll unchecked through them both knowing that, win or lose, everything in the future is going to change.

The onyx and black marble of his citadel entrance looms large and dark, the sight sending a shiver running through her. But Reyanne will not be entering through the front gate, nor will she be running through the sewers. She will wait until sunrise and perform her specialty—turning into a ball of light to find her way to Zanthrand's chambers overlooking the city from on high. He awaits her there, tense and pacing.

Dawn? he asks.

She nods, unseen, though he can sense her agreement anyway. *Do you think we'll feel one another die?*

Perhaps, he says. *Or perhaps your soul-bond may be the ruin of us. No matter who is killed, both our lives might drain away. How ironic. Where will that leave our armies then?*

There's no answer to that. It's just a risk Reyanne will have to take.

The sky turns pink at the ridge of the horizon. As soon as the first rays of sunlight touch her, Reyanne can perform her spell, and perform it, she does. Being shapeless in the ether is the best feeling in Reyanne's difficult life. It's the only time she feels free from her burdens. Free from responsibilities. Sometimes she wishes she could just dissipate, but no such luck ever finds her.

Come to me, he calls.

She couldn't stay away if she tried.

His sill is ornate with gargoyles and angels in constant struggle, his internal battle for light and dark illustrated in marble. Reyanne suffers the same imbalance, though the darkness in her remains repressed in a bottle that grows by the day. One that begs to be opened even as she stoppers it, the same way he boxes away his light, sealing it in a tomb. Just like his dead master, Zanthrand will not allow it to rule him.

When she lands, she goes to her knees momentarily on his cold, stone floor. The transformation always leaves her weak, no matter how many times she does it. He stands over her, looking down, every muscle tight. She's been traveling for days, but they've never discussed what happens now.

"Now you sleep," he says. "Rest and replenish your magic."

"That seems like a stupid idea."

"Then call me a fool. There is no winner today if I don't best you properly."

"Still assuming you'll win?"

He offers a hand to help her up. "One way or the other."

Unease fills her breast. "And no one knows I'm here?"

"Now who's the fool?" he asks. "Did you think I'd bring my army down on your head?"

Uncaring of its timing, her stomach grumbles and she shrinks back to cover it sheepishly.

"You'll also eat." He leans down to grab her arm now, pulling her up roughly. "Meat, as well. No arguments."

She grumps. She doesn't like eating animals.

"Yes, well. Get your strength up. Last meal and all that," he says.

"Then make it something I like."

He sighs but is otherwise unmoved. Walking deeper into his chambers, she follows. They are larger than hers by far, auspicious with several rooms, a dining room included. It's almost intimate in size, though. She had expected a banquet hall but sees only a table for four.

"Why four?"

He looks longingly at the beautifully carved chairs and fine, polished wood. "It's a wish for something beyond solitude."

It pangs her heart. Clearing her throat, she continues to follow behind. He pulls back heavy curtains to show a bathing room complete with a deep tub of steaming water. Oils and soaps abound.

"For you. Food will be waiting by the time you finish. Then sleep."

"The end comes tonight, then?" she asks.

He agrees. "Tonight."

Without another word, Reyanne steps into the room and the heavy curtain closes behind her. Her clothes are dirty and worn through, yet on a washstand, she sees a new set left behind for her. The style looks similar to her own, but in absolute black.

Seriously? she sends him.

Beggars can't be choosers, Reyanne.

She huffs as she strips, easing herself into the nearly scalding water, a luxury she's never had. Idly, she wonders what the Separatists think of her escape. They likely know she came to do this alone and must be keeping hushed to avoid tipping off the Dark Moon to her presence, in case she was planning a sneak attack.

Nonsense. You'd never do that, he grumbles in her mind. *It's like they don't even know you.*

Not surprising. No one does.

His words are soft. *I do...*

It causes an uncomfortable flutter in her heart; one she dismisses immediately. "Get out of my head and leave me alone. Otherwise, how can I wash properly?"

He snorts from a small distance, moving further away. It's all she can really ask for, given she can never truly escape him. Not until tonight. One way or the other.

* * *

Reyanne lies in his luxurious furs, the skin of each hide tanned to a satiny softness. The rest of his room is cold, but this space is warm and...dare she say...inviting. She comes to awareness slowly, Zanthrand lying beside her just as he has many times through the mirror gate. He's still deep asleep, also gathering his magic, and his face looks peaceful. The deep mark from his forehead to cheek looks oddly becoming, and she longs to run a finger over it. Perhaps to kiss it. She can't think thoughts like this when he's awake.

I'll have to come at him from his blindside, she decides, though she'll also need to firm up another ten or more strategies to keep him on his toes when he opens up to read her mind during battle.

Looking at him, she could end him now, but one could say they've given each other a professional courtesy, offering peace and respite until their final confrontation...though Reyanne knows better. They're delaying the inevitable, neither truly wanting the other to die. She knows they both fear the killing blow as much as whatever consequences may follow, even if the only consequence is loneliness.

Zanthrand is bare from the waist up and his scars show like designs over his muscular curves. He's defenseless like this and she's more than happy to stare.

I'd wanted to be in a man's arms...what about his?

She needs to stop. She doesn't indulge in fantasies like

this and cannot afford to start now. Not with as gentle as he looks, lips slightly parted as he breathes.

He's evil, Reyanne reminds herself. *He's a monster.*

But the words seem hollow. Thrusting herself out of bed, she paces, her angry huffs finally rousing him.

"I'm not ready yet," he mumbles, turning over and nestling deep under his blankets.

"You're going to drive me mad!"

"Enjoy what may be your last night alive, my white witch. Take what pleasure you can, even if only in good food, hot water, a warm bed, and good company."

She scoffs. "Get up."

"No."

"Get. Up."

He digs deeper in, snuggling, and her temper boils over. Stomping closer, she pulls the furs off, exposing him to the chill and seeing his skin prickle. It does something to her insides, and she looks away.

"Don't drag this out," she says. It's a plea without outright begging.

With a heavy sigh, he begins to rise, shuffling around as emotions build up inside him…ones that turn to utter rage. With a deep grunt, he begins to topple various objects; crashes and clangs reverberate off the arched stone walls, filling the empty space with noise. Reyanne whips around to see ceramic flying, side tables smashing, his bed being ripped to shreds, all by Zanthrand's own hand. His teeth show as he growls at nothing other than the situation, losing his mind in short bursts.

It's over in moments, though it's burned a forever-picture in Reyanne's brain.

Zanthrand rakes his fingers through his hair as he pants roughly, nostrils flaring, but otherwise acts as if nothing happened. He doesn't look at her. She doesn't know if she wants him to. He's terrifying in this moment. Feral. She's going to die tonight, isn't she?

"Don't fight me, Reyanne," he says. "Go. Or stay. But don't fight me tonight."

Stubborn, she shakes her head. "It's now or never."

"Can't we choose never?" He sounds like a child, mulish and sulking.

Taking his hand, Reyanne yanks, pulling him to the central training area in his chambers. His weapons and hers lay atop one another as if they were old friends…or something more. Bending down, she picks up what belongs to him and shoves it into his arms. He's not wearing anything in the way of protection for his upper body, but he'll either have to make do or get himself sorted quickly. He'll have to…

Zanthrand drops his weapon and grabs Reyanne around the waist as she walks away. In a mere second, he's pulled her close, her back pressing up against his hard body. One hand locks around her ribcage and the other slips under her arm and takes her by the throat—but gently. Attention seeking. Needy.

"Don't fight me," he says again. "Please."

She's going to melt against him. Her lungs work too fast, dragging in little gulps of air and letting her throat work against the flat of his palm. "A-afraid to lose?"

"I won't lose."

"Stop underestimating me!" she hisses as she struggles against him.

"I've divined it. I know what will happen and I know I won't be able to stop myself. One way or another, Reyanne, you will be mine tonight. Whether in life or in death is up to you."

His lips caress the curve of her neck, his hot breath making her knees weak.

"What are you doing?" she asks.

"Wanting you," he murmurs. The hand that rested on her stomach slides up to palm a breast before landing over her thrumming heart. "Desiring you." His calloused thumb traces her jawline. "Offering to be the man that loves you."

She's going to burst. Whether into flames or into tears, she doesn't know. She's going to hyperventilate. Down his hand goes again, trailing between her breasts, over her stomach, and coming to rest between her legs.

"Let me love you, Reyanne. Make my wish come true. Be my something more."

Dear reader, does Reyanne:
Reject Zanthrand's affection, turn to page 51 (chapter 10)
Give in, turn to page 55 (chapter 11)

CHAPTER 10

Reyanne rears forward, dislodging herself from his grip before angling around to face him. "You're trying to trick me. Distract me. I'm no fool, Zanthrand."

He slides his fingers through his soft hair to reveal his temple in invitation. "Look into my mind. See the truth."

"No," she growls. "I came here for only one thing."

His lips press together as rejection flows through their bond, replaced quickly by a simmering anger on the verge of boiling. "I told you that I win."

"The arrogance!" Reyanne sneers at him. "I'm more powerful than you think!"

With a sigh, he closes his eyes. "So be it."

His arm drifts out to the side as his lips whisper, calling his weapon into his hand with a snap. He unsheathes the black blade, a moving, red miasma winding endlessly around it, just as roiling as his emotions inside. They swell beyond anger. Beyond rage. Zanthrand feels like nothing but hate, his good eye tinged with the violent color of his weapon, making him look like a true demon.

"Arm yourself," he says. "Or don't."

With that, he dives forward with a harsh jab.

Reyanne pulls out of the way only just in time, the blade searing her skin and making her cry out. She lunges for her staff, skidding on her knees and whipping around to catch his downstroke.

"We're going to destroy your room," she says, trying to weave in their familiar banter as she struggles to hold his blade at bay.

His voice is made of ice as he echoes himself. "So be it."

The pressure of his weight lays into her, making her muscles tremble. Spells flick through her mind in rapid succession to ensure he can't read what she's doing until the last minute when she chants, "Ka'rosh indeigo allain itoshi."

The air crystallizes around them, frigid as the world's north and south poles. Zanthrand's breath plumes white while Reyanne remains in a bubble of warmth, unfazed and uncowed. The room fills with clouds of white mist, and she knows it must be biting cold, based on his stance…yet he only smiles.

Lips falling into a sneer, he hisses, "Ssshatha," and a bright ring of flames roars around them, undoing Reyanne's spell with one word.

She ducks out from under his weapon, letting Zanthrand fall forward, using his weight against him. There is a sharp, metallic *clunk* as his blade embeds in the floor, melting the stone into black glass, as if the polished material was only sand. When she wins, Reyanne will take that pretty material and string a dark necklace of both victory and mourning, wearing it under her armor at all times, its meaning known to her alone.

Reyanne leaps to her feet and mutters a single word, making it rain in heavy sheets, tamping down the blaze. Zanthrand's dappled hair reflects the light as the vestiges of fire throw embers into the air. He looks beautiful. Stunning.

Like a wild animal. He comes at her in fast steps, making her retreat on her tiptoes.

Agile, Reyanne reminds herself. Her one advantage against his massive body. She dashes in with a purposefully predictable swipe of her staff, and when he goes to block it, she pivots, slicing through his side in a shallow gash. He doesn't even flinch. He only smirks at her, his one good eye as black as night.

Hair clinging to his forehead, he angles his blade, words drip-dropping from his lips as the stone floor beneath them begins to rumble.

Her calves tense and her ankles lock tight, her balance at work as she leaves her knees loose, riding the waves of rock like one would a dragon whose wings pump in wide circles of pure muscle.

"Indaga kirrith la'ankaht," she tries, taking full blocks from the floor and raising them up in the air, held on nothing but her thoughts. She needs to create a barrier of obstacles between Zanthrand and herself if she wants her chance at winning.

She catches glimpses of him behind the floating stones as she dodges and weaves, leaping up to flit from one to the other in acrobatic steps and jumps. Zanthrand doesn't waste his energy trying to match her. Instead, as she lunges downward with her unsheathed golden blade stabbing toward him. He dodges only slightly, taking a hit to the shoulder...

...before ramming his blade through her stomach, all the way to the pommel.

Reyanne is close enough to kiss him. Blood fills her lungs before her wound cauterizes around the fiery blade his weapon has ruined her with.

Neither haughty nor triumphant, instead his voice sounds strangled. "I told you."

The rocks come tumbling down as his weapon moves its

way easily through her left side, melting her ribcage with no effort. With a single word, his blade shuts off and he tosses the hilt aside mindlessly, getting to his knees beside her. She can't breathe. Her chest rises and falls, but there isn't enough oxygen to sustain her. A fish on the chopping block, she tries to struggle, but he shushes her, resting a hand on her hip to still her futile scrambling.

He leans down and kisses her forehead. Each of her eyes. Her bloodied lips.

"My hope dies with you," he tells her. "As do your Separatists."

Reyanne knows it's the utter truth. Her pride has killed them all.

"Zan—" she tries, but he rests his fingertips over her mouth, and all other words slip away.

I loved you, he whispers into her mind.

I know, she returns.

And then the world goes black.

You, dear reader, have earned a <u>SAD ENDING</u>!

Remember, there are 17 possible endings, and this is just one. If you've found all nine Reyanne endings, start back at the beginning, and choose Zanthrand's path. Many diverging stories await you!

Good luck, dear reader!

CHAPTER 11

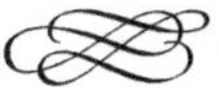

"No one's ever loved me," Reyanne whispers, feeling the warmth of a kiss placed just under her ear. Her first one.

She begins to tremble. *Even as a child, I was abandoned. Alone. Afraid.*

"I could never abandon you," he sighs the words along the shell of her ear. "You are my world. Whether hating you or longing for you, you take over my senses."

His fingers curl between her thighs and she gasps, resulting in a low hum and a swell of his pride.

"My family rejected me, too," he tells her. "But since you've tied us together, I've never been alone." His hand tightens on her throat, pinning her in place. "Please don't make me be alone."

He sinks his teeth into the space between her neck and her shoulder, and her knees buckle. He holds her up, though, that physical prowess of his unyielding. She feels like a boneless doll, one he treats with gentleness and reverence.

"Why didn't I feel these emotions in you?" she asks, her voice nearly gone.

"It's my biggest secret. My biggest weakness. I buried it under anger the way you bury yours under fear. But I heard you, Reyanne. I hear you now." His voice drops low, "I *feel* you now."

And his curled fingers between her legs hike up higher, pressing deliciously on a part of her body she didn't even know she had.

"Zan," she whines an intimate name for him, something she's never done. It's embarrass—

"Shh," he commands, licking a stripe up her pulse point. "Say it again."

He suckles her earlobe and dances his fingers down below. More than saying his name, she moans it, and he growls his excitement in return.

"Do you know what that does to me?" he asks. The heel of his hand presses the flat of her belly, pulling her backwards at the same time his hips tip up, something hard riding against the top of her rear. She squeaks, and he chuckles. "Know what that is, my white witch?"

She can feel his body like a blaze, both from the heat of him grinding against her, and another strange, phantom sensation of pleasure in a part of her body that doesn't exist. It's like she's living in his body in the same way she's living in her own.

In a quick movement, he catches her in his arms, lifting her and stepping back toward where his bed awaits. He mutters an incantation, and floating pyre lights burst into flame, surrounding the wooden bedframe on all sides, radiating warmth to soothe Reyanne's chilled skin.

"We shouldn't…" she tries, but her legs tip open instinctively.

He stares up from between her ankles, his one eye gleaming. "Don't talk. Just feel, princess."

And, oh, how that name sends a flare of desire up her

body. She's always wanted to be important like that. To be seen. To be cared for.

"And care for you, I will." Zanthrand dives down between her legs, pressing his mouth against the black clothes he'd gifted her. Even through the fabric, the heat of his breath makes her yelp. She wants more. She needs it. Craves it.

He pulls back and hooks his fingers under the hem of her pants, yanking down to reveal her body to the firelight. Reyanne tries to curl in on herself, ashamed, but there's no time for that. He drives forward again, his pale hands digging into the flesh of her inner thighs as he pins them open, his mouth even hotter as it lands on her center and suckles.

"Gods!" she cries out, unable to help herself.

I love your taste, he sends to her. *Like salt and sugar and something unnamable. Something that's just you. You're like ambrosia, princess. I'm going to drink you like wine.*

Something clenches inside her as his tongue flicks. Her hands plunge into his hair, and he gasps against her.

Grip tight, sweet thing. Hold me close. Don't let me pull an inch away. I need to get you ready.

"Ready for wh—?" she starts but is shocked into a squeak when something slips inside her. It's his finger, ever so slightly nudging in circles.

Licking a hot stripe, he presses deeper. "Lucky all your horse riding broke you in."

Dragon riding, she can't help but correct, and she feels his amusement carry over through their bond.

He focuses on her apex, sucking while his finger undulates, and Reyanne doesn't know what to do with herself. She bites the back of her fist, trying to ground herself before she dies from his touches. She's burning up. Her belly tenses and her toes splay.

That's it, princess. Give it to me.

Give what?

Your pleasure.

And Reyanne ignites. Something inside her spasms, and her magic lashes out, shattering the only glass bowl Zanthrand hadn't already destroyed. Still his finger works, joined by a second now, pumping in and out of her, making the feeling last.

"Zan, please," she begs, and his motions slow. He pants, pressing kisses over her belly.

"Gods, I *felt* that…" He sounds ruined, and it makes Reyanne want more. She wants his fingers moving again. Even more than that. Everything.

Each and every scrap of his clothes comes off before he scrabbles for her tunic. She is too euphoric to complain as he lifts the rough fabric and follows her down, wrapping his tongue around her nipple and groaning.

"I'm going insane," he whispers. "I'm never coming back from this."

This time, it's the outer frame of his legs that pins hers apart as he rides the outside of her, slick and hot. He's hitting that perfect place again, but Reyanne can also feel him teetering on the edge of something. His own precipice. Knowing what it is now, she suddenly wants *his* pleasure more than she'd wanted her own.

Hooking her heels, she notches him against her in one stroke, and his mouth drops open, jaw slack.

"Kiss me," she says.

It seems to dawn on him only now that he hasn't yet, and he gives her mouth the same attention that he did the rest of her. Reyanne tugs his hips closer once more and he begins to open her completely, making him lose his concentration and moan against her mouth. Reyanne won't let up, easing him in and feeling his length fill her up inch by inch. At the same time, she also feels his sensation…her body forming a vise-like grip around him, wet and hot.

This is unimaginable. This is unbelievable.

This makes her insatiable.

Pivoting her body during his weak moment, she flips them both, putting herself on top as she sinks onto him, tears standing out in her eyes. It not just the sting. It's not just the overwhelming stimulation. It's the feeling of being whole. Of being one.

She never wants this to end.

He looks desperate beneath her as his one eye travels from her face down the rest of her body, fixating on where they join. Grabbing her hips a bit too hard, he guides her up, biting his lip as he watches himself pull out and hissing in a breath when she takes him back in.

There is such power to be had here. Just as much as in battle. More. Because he's giving in to her willingly.

She wants to eat him alive.

Her body rocks against him, finding not only where it's the most comfortable, but the way it feels the absolute best. She throws her head back as his hands travel her body, sensual curses falling from between his clenched teeth. He won't last long, and she can feel it. She wants it to go on forever, but she doesn't. She needs him to stay, but she needs him to explode.

"Please, Zan." She rocks harder. Faster. "I need it."

And he rips over the edge, bringing Reyanne with him. Still, she grinds with abandon; she pulses around him; she repeats the word *yes* like it's the only word she knows.

Wrapping a hand around her upper back, he tugs her forward, bringing them chest to chest as he takes her mouth again.

Stay with me, he pleads. *Be mine. Never leave. Make me whole.*

Thoughts swirl in Reyanne's head. Yes. No. She wants to

run. She wants him inside her forever. She needs to destroy him. She needs to adore him.

But which will she do?

Dear reader, does Reyanne:
Remember her duty, turn to page 61 (chapter 12)

Realize she needs to be with him at all costs, turn to page 66 (chapter 13)

CHAPTER 12

"*I* can't..." Reyanne says quietly, her mouth hovering just over his.

Shock grips him, and something in his chest breaks open, matching Reyanne's pain note for note. "Still going to kill me, then?"

Reyanne shakes her head, her fingers digging into his shoulders as she doesn't know quite how to move. "Are *you* going to kill *me?*"

He looks at her. Just looks. "I don't know *what* to do with you." In a quick movement, he rolls her off with a *thump* and stands, balling his fists and taking in the destruction he'd wrought earlier, objects strewn around the bed frame like jagged trash.

"Leave."

"What?"

"*Now,*" he growls.

Reyanne looks away, trying to cover herself as he bends down, tossing her clothes back at her. Walking away, he rubs his hands over his face as if scrubbing away all emotion.

"Zan," she tries.

"I should have killed you." He pauses, his strong back facing her. Turning over his shoulder he admits, "I should have let you kill me."

In her mind, she overhears his thoughts, the words unintended for her. His mind is on repeat: *This wasn't enough. It will never be enough.*

Reyanne doesn't know what to say. Nothing comes. But the sunlight does, and it touches her skin as a promise of escape.

He's walking away. He hurts and she hurts and why does it have to be like this?

Her lips trembling, Reyanne bursts into tears before saying her spell and turning back into a ball of white light. She sees all angles like this, a 360-degree view of all things. Through it, she watches Zanthrand throw over a piece of furniture, then another...but it's too late to stay.

* * *

Osric meets Reyanne at the gate to the castle, his face stern with fury. "You left."

She can't meet his eyes. "And I failed."

The man breathes in deeply before sighing out a rough puff of air. "No. You survived. That means we still have a chance. As long as you're alive, we can beat him. You're our only hope, Reyanne. I know you can do this."

Osric reaches around and puts an arm over her shoulder to lead her inside. Reyanne's soul howls with emotion, and she feels Zanthrand echo her pain on the other side of their bond.

Why did she give in to him? She had hidden from her feelings before, but there's no controlling this now. How can she face him? How can the Separatists expect her to…hurt him?

She can't. Remembering the amber of his eyes and his mouth on hers, remembering being treated like she matters as more than just a weapon, remembering his four chairs and his hidden, sweet wish for a family, Reyanne could never, ever kill the Dark Moon.

That leaves only one option.

Despair floods her. She hides her thoughts behind memories of his body, his words, and his secret dreams of something more, afraid to let him see what she's about to do. She's almost grateful he's somewhere destroying something. It means that by the time he realizes what's happening, it will be too late.

* * *

The concoction Reyanne has whipped up is hot in her hands. It's reacting badly with the clear vial, causing smoke to rise, viscous and deadly. Still, it shouldn't hurt. She feels Zanthrand's injuries, he feels hers, and the last thing she wants is to bring him more pain. That's why she's doing it like this.

Grimly, Reyanne stares at her clenched fist. She is resolved from her brain to her gut, no matter the fear, no matter the anguish. It's the fear that gets his attention, she thinks, because he rampages over like a storm, digging through her mind's nooks and crannies, making her wince and cry out from leagues away.

What are you up to, my white witch? The possessive word in his question screams at her, even though he feels filled with hate.

Quickly, before he realizes, Reyanne opens her throat and downs the poison. It sits in her belly for only moments before her head feels light.

She can sense the very moment Zanthrand understands what she's done. It's like his whole body goes cold.

The portal tears open, then. Not the mirror gate, where he couldn't lay a hand on her if he tried, but the actual portal, its rending rip sending Zanthrand into her space like a nightmare she longs for.

"What have you done?" he asks, his one eye open wide.

Reyanne goes to her knees, her palms slapping the marble floor beneath her as the vial clatters uselessly to the side. "It will be quick. I…I don't want it to hurt you."

"And if it kills me? If I die with you?"

She shakes her head. "I don't want that either."

She reels and starts to fall back, but he catches her, his black garb spreading on the floor like a midnight pool.

"We have to neutralize it," he says.

Reyanne feels him raking roughly through her mind, snatching the list of her ingredients. But the antidotes are too rare, and he knows it. Stammering, he tries, "I…I can make you sick. Rid your body of it—"

She rests her hand over his. "Or you could let me go."

And a tear falls. Just one. But one tear from Zanthrand is like a waterfall.

He brings her up to his chest, folding her in his arms, squeezing all too tight. "Why would you do this?"

"B-because…I can't…I can't kill you. I won't."

"Reyanne…" It's like his voice is broken.

She forces herself to pull back, watching the tears he's weeping now as if they're jewels. Her vision is getting hazy. It doesn't hurt at all. It's like falling asleep. "Tell me…you can't feel it."

He grabs her hand and rests it over his cheek. "No, princess. I can't."

She smiles just the tiniest bit. "Good. Then m-maybe... you'll..." but it's hard to talk right now. It's hard to make her mouth move.

His sob makes her fall in love with him all the more. She pushes that feeling to him through their bond.

"Don't leave," he begs her, his words coming fast. "Please, Reyanne. Without you..."

Without me, this war will end, she thinks. *Without me, you'll finally be safe.*

Her mind goes quiet. No matter how much Zanthrand weeps and pleads, those words are the last thing Reyanne ever thinks.

The world has gone black.

You, dear reader, have earned a <u>SAD ENDING</u>!

Remember, there are 17 possible endings, and this is just one. If you've found all nine Reyanne endings, start back at the beginning, and choose Zanthrand's path. Many diverging stories await you!

Good luck, dear reader!

CHAPTER 13

"I'll stay," she says against his lips before dipping in again, swirling her tongue over his, but the desperation of the act calms as he begins to caress her, slow and tender. Hopeful.

Don't tease me, princess.

She smiles against his mouth. "…But only if…"

He grunts, though he doesn't stop kissing her.

You said you'd share your power. Your status. Make me your equal, Zanthrand, she says.

He grabs the meaty part of her rear and hikes her up against him as he hardens again. "And what would you do with your newfound prowess, hm?"

She answers him honestly. "End the war."

He narrows his eye at her, his emotions sinking into a familiar anger. "I believe in order through a firm hand. I will not abide by the Separatists, whether or not one lies in my bed."

Reyanne swallows. She's not Separatist. Not anymore. Perhaps if the Separatists fell, the fighting would stop. Perhaps if the fighting stopped, the conditions for the

Dominion territories would improve…or perhaps she'd be in a position to make it so. "What if I gave you access to their leadership the next time our portal opens?"

Everything about him stops. His breath, his movement. "You lie."

She rests her head on his chest, fleeing his regard. "Feel me. You think I would lie about this?"

Reyanne shares her trepidation and fear. The sickness in her stomach at the very idea of breaking with the Separatists. They've been with her all this time and have kept her close, though at arm's length as well. She is a weapon to them, even if their most precious. She's never been anything more than that.

"You would betray them?"

"It's either that…or betray you." Her tears roll over his pectoral muscle and into the valley that dips to his collarbone.

"You came here to kill me…"

"Yet instead, I loved you."

Joy fills Zanthrand from the bottom to the top, his feelings overwhelming Reyanne's uncertainty. He tamps it down with a wary paranoia after only a moment. "You're using me."

"Yes… And no. I'm using both of us to build a better future. But only if…"

He sighs this time, annoyed. "If what?"

She curls in tighter. "If you promise to love me forever."

And it's like he melts. His fingertips slide over her back and up to her neck. Slipping his fingers under her jaw, he lifts her eyes to his, holding her there. An awe relaxes his features into something absolutely stunning.

Caressing the crest of her cheek, he says, "Forever isn't nearly long enough, princess."

He kisses her again, sweetly, softly, whispering his heart's deepest wish into her mind.

And soon to be...my queen.

You, dear reader, have earned a <u>HAPPY ENDING</u>!
The only one in the Reyanne track! Good job, you!

Remember, there are 17 possible endings, and this is just one. If you've found all nine Reyanne endings, start back at the beginning, and choose Zanthrand's path. Many diverging stories await you!

Good luck, dear reader!

CHAPTER 14

*E*xcitement. A thrill runs up her spine, prickling her skin into gooseflesh. She feels all too clearly where his hand grips her hair and revels in the tug of it. It lights a fire within her.

"M-maybe," Reyanne says evenly despite a flare of pain up her side, her wound aching and stinging. "Maybe I don't want to escape."

Everything about Zanthrand freezes.

"Maybe I'm just as obsessed as you are…" The admission fills her with a shame just as strong as her desire.

He edges closer, his nose caressing hers. "Don't tease, Reyanne. You wouldn't like it if I took you seriously."

"We'll see," she whispers, closing the distance and kissing him. It hurts his wound—she can feel her own face suddenly ache with his pain—but that doesn't stop him from returning her passion, taking her mouth until they're both breathless.

Reyanne's knees buckle, and he follows her to the ground, holding her despite the myriad of torn pieces of flesh along his arms and chest. Something within him hungers so deeply, Reyanne can feel it burn her from the inside out as his tongue touches hers. A heavy, deep sound rumbles from his chest, sending a tingle racing through her.

"Zan," she whispers against him as he hovers, catching his breath. "We can't."

"Too late for that, my darling. Far, far too late."

One last kiss sends Reyanne spiraling into unconsciousness, one she's glad to surrender to. He pulls her mind down, down, down to darkness and peace—which is for the best, because she doesn't know whether to submit completely or start fighting again, and either choice has its consequences.

* * *

Reyanne awakens in a room of cavernous stone; one she knows well.

Zanthrand's chambers.

The bond between them works in strange ways. Beyond sharing minds and sensations, the connection also opens what they've started to call a "mirror gate"—a wide, oval-shaped window that hovers in the air, its edges fading off into nowhere. Through it they can see each other, speak to each other, scream at each other…but they can never touch. Worse, though, is when the fabric of reality rips open to create a portal, putting them in the same space. Sometimes he in hers, sometimes she in his. That's when their battles are truly fought, far away from the prying eyes of the armies that usually stand behind them.

She recognizes Zanthrand's living space, his warm bed in warm colors, a stark contrast to the man who is ever drenched in black. This isn't a vision or a magic trick…it's real.

He lies beside her now, his own dreamland owning him.

Dark scabs are the only thing holding his wounds together, and Reyanne can tell his bad eye will never see again. She's the one who did it to him, but it gives her no sense of satisfaction.

Being here is horrible. Terrible. Not only a betrayal of her people, but she also feels like—

"A mouse about to be eaten," he mumbles half asleep, completing her sentence. "Whereas I feel like a fool about to be betrayed. That's what's in your mind, isn't it? After all your sinful touches, you still want to run home to the people who would kill you for such treachery."

He's not wrong. When it comes to her mind, he is never wrong.

Reyanne's hand goes to the wound on her side. It's been treated, but it still aches.

"You've hidden us away," she whispers. "None of your people must know you brought me here or we would have been healed already. Either that, or I'd be dead."

"Or perhaps I just killed anyone who stood in the way of me capturing my white witch and decided keeping you weak was the best way to keep you tame."

"Liar."

His lips quirk up at the sides.

"But we need to be taken care of," she says. "Otherwise—"

"We won't be able to fight each other." He frowns. "You still want to kill me, then? Now's your time. I won't argue. I got a taste of you I'd never thought I'd have; it would be romantic to die in your arms. But a warning: end me here and my people will destroy you. And then I'll see you in hell, Reyanne—for as much blood as we have on our hands, we'll both be there."

"And the devil will keep us close, but still at arm's length for all eternity, just to torture us."

Zanthrand's face blooms into a full smile, making him

look young. "And being kept that far from me would be torture?"

His hand slides up Reyanne's arm and she notices he's stripped his outer regalia, leaving only a frayed black tunic, sliced and rigid with dried blood.

Reyanne's hand comes up over his.

"Stop."

He narrows his good eye at her. "And why would I ever do that?"

"You'll open your wounds."

"I don't give a damn about my wounds."

To make a point, he hoists himself up and over Reyanne's body, pressing his weight on her chest and kissing her again, even as she can feel his pain. His lips are soft despite the firmness of the rest of him, the weight on her almost suffocating, yet lighting her ablaze.

Stop, she begs again into his mind.

"I can't," he whispers over her. "You've broken a dam, my darling, and now I'll drown you in me."

Her hand goes up, her fingers slipping through the dark hair at his temple…and he sighs. It's not a happy sound. It's resigned.

"Do it, then," he says.

And Reyanne uses her magic to put him to immediate sleep. She cries out when he goes limp on top of her, even heavier now in his slumber. "I'm sorry. I'm so sorry." She chants it like it matters, even though she knows it doesn't.

She can't do this. She can't be this person. She can't be trapped in his vortex—which, make no mistake, is exactly what he is. He's a murk of passion, power, strength, and need. She's always attributed those things only to his desire to win the war, but it seems she missed the mark. Though, to be fair, she'd refused to face those emotions in herself, as well. Until now.

She presses kisses onto his face as if branding her regret and conflict into his skin. She could kill him now. Perhaps he thought she would. But she can no sooner do that than she can stay with him.

Then it dawns on her.

"You told me you'd go to the ends of the earth to find me." She presses her forehead to his. "In this, I'll trust you."

With that, Reyanne extracts herself from beneath him and stands, wobbling on her feet a little, but feeling her magic has returned again. Rest has done her wonders. She hums a few notes before diving into incantations that she can feel, her wound sealing. She draws symbols in the air that hang there, etched in white sparks and surrounded by a blue glow. Once her drawn circle is complete, the runes swirl and fly into her chest, warming every part of her and restoring her vitality, eliminating any toxins that found their way into her blood.

Turning around, she whispers another spell over Zanthrand, caressing his lips and sliding her finger down the meridian of his body. Her hands travel over his breastbone, down his abdomen, over his hidden navel as healing words pour from her lips. His gashes and lacerations knit closed… though she can't fix his eye. For that, she can never atone.

"I love you," she says. "I've always loved you. And that's why I hated you. Because I knew in my heart it would always come to this."

She can't go home, not with this feeling finally laid bare within her. It's a bleeding heart that will never heal.

Her part in the war is not yet over, though. If his obsession for her is true, then he will look for her. Distracted, he will make a mistake. Then, the Separatists will find their much-needed chink in the Dominion's armor.

"Survive when they come for you. Please." She pushes his hair back from his forehead, a slow caress. "And please find me when your world comes tumbling down."

With that, Reyanne kisses him one last time, her falling tears cleaning the soot of war off his cheeks.

It's time to go.

* * *

Reyanne looks out across an overgrown field, shielding her eyes from the sun. It's been two years since she cut off her magic, which severed the bond. Every day it hurts, but magic is not the only thing Reyanne has given up in her new life.

She barely ventures into town, avoiding any news of conflict as if it would destroy her to hear one side has won over the other. Or worse somehow, that the battle still rages on. She keeps to herself, farming and building small greenhouses around her homestead. It's so remote here that no one comes to see her, and therefore no one knows of the stores of food she's been growing during the ongoing famine. With or without magic, she still can perform miracles.

There are many dreams and nightmares that haunt her, but the one that lingers long past daybreak is the fear that she'd doomed him, her unattainable lover. Somehow, even the thought of betraying her comrades pales in comparison to this ache in her soul.

She wants him to find her, and the feeling grows stronger the more time passes. Until then, she counts the days.

Often, so often, she's tempted to call back her magic. To touch his mind. To beg the mirror gate to open so that she might see his face—preferably while he would be sleeping, but one could never know with him. He was a beast that prowled at all hours.

Still, one day she knows she'll give in despite the risks and consequences. As long as he's alive, he'll sweep in like a whirlwind and take her. She *wants* him to take her. But will he even be there when she dares to look?

And so, her internal tally takes on new meaning. She's either counting down to the fated day she finds she's truly alone, or to the day she decides to join him, dark magic or not. Dominion or not. He's seducing her even in his absence.

"I miss him," she tells the blue sky.

It's only a matter of time.

You, dear reader, have earned an <u>OPEN ENDING</u>!

Remember, there are 17 possible endings, and this is just one. If you've found all nine Reyanne endings, start back at the beginning, and choose Zanthrand's path. Many diverging stories await you!

Good luck, dear reader!

CHAPTER 15

Reyanne lets herself fall to her knees once more, dropping her staff and letting it ricochet off the ground in a clatter, a sharp, ringing sound she can't bring herself to care about. She's exhausted. She's hurt. She's bleeding profusely and yet she shut off her call for help, all to sit with her most fitful nightmare. Her darkest dream.

"I want you to tell me that I'm not nothing." She puts her face in her hands and lets out a harsh sob. Her brain tingles with Zanthrand's thoughts, but she can't wrap her mind around anything beyond her own overwhelming sorrow and regret.

"I'll never be what you want me to be," he says quietly… but she can't place his tone. Is he angry? Or is he something else?

A familiar chanting begins, a spell she'd recognize anywhere, and Reyanne shakes her head in her hands.

"Don't do this. Don't go. Please."

"You and I, Reyanne," his voice has a whispering quality as it begins to fade at the edges, "will only ever be enemies. It's fate. Destiny. Written in the stars. Our choices have been made for us it seems. Though, perhaps…" His voice trails off, but his words ring on in her mind.

Perhaps in another life, we could have been so much more…

The smell of ozone floods the canyon, the tell-tale scent of Zanthrand becoming dark smoke and escaping, as he has done many, many times. He can only achieve this at night, just as Reyanne can only transform into a ball of light during the day. She runs from him just as often as he runs from her.

Normally, when Zanthrand slips past her in a murky blur, she is beyond vengeful. But now? Now she is crushed… because she knows he feels it too. This pull. This longing.

His dark haze cools her cheek as it passes, drying her trail of tears, though the feeling of him only adds to her sorrow.

"REYANNE!" a familiar voice suddenly screams from above.

Reyanne rears her head back, taking in the sky. A dragon rider swoops overhead, blotting out the moon before spiraling down through the canyon. The crevasse is dark, but the Separatists' pale clothes should glimmer and stand out next to the strewn bodies of Dominion black. The trick is finding her in this sea of the dead.

"Osric…" she tries, but it comes out weak. Feeble. She can't hold on. For now, her power is drained, leaving her empty.

And Reyanne collapses to the ground.

* * *

"Open your eyes…"

Reyanne blinks slowly. Njal Osric is casting charms over her, his warm brown hands moving in fluid motions to create the Druid symbols of healing. Glowing blue, they swim in the air, their sigils being drawn in lightning white with every guttural syllable he utters. Reyanne's side throbs and itches, a tell-tale sign that he's either doing it very right, or very wrong.

Her fellow magic-caster has brought her to the castle's apothecary, which doubles as a magician's medical station. Bottles of every color line tables and shelves. Books are strewn about haphazardly, precious and rare and loved, but nuisances nonetheless when there is work to be done that requires the much-coveted table space. Large tapestries the color of cream and ivory play host to the bright red Separatists' insignia, a moon-like crescent that blooms into crystalline shapes at the low point of its curve—the exact inverse of the Dominion's black banner. They drape down the stone walls at the cardinal points of north, south, east, and west, ensuring everyone knows exactly where their loyalties lie, no matter what direction they face.

Lavender and thyme are being crushed together into a calming powder as Lilah Tai, a young woman with almond eyes and straight black hair, runs a pestle around the bottom of a marble bowl. It makes a familiar scraping sound, bringing to memory all the years Reyanne has spent in this room making potions and predictions, medicines and miracles.

"There you are," Osric says through a grin. "I thought we'd lost you."

"You almost did," Reyanne admits, sinking back into the feather down blanket that softens the pallet below her.

"What happened?" Lilah asks. "No one else survived the campaign. Not even General Pike."

With a final few hand gestures, Osric's blue symbols swirl around in the air, spiraling into a white light that merges with Reyanne's wound, setting it to complete rights.

"I'll tell you what happened," Osric scowls. "Zanthrand happened."

"War happened," Reyanne corrects.

"It's all that ever does." Lilah sighs. "And it's all those damn Dominion soldiers deserve, too. If every last one of us goes down, at least we'll go down fighting. I'd rather die than see even one of the Dark Moon's spawn crawl their way off the battlefield."

And yesterday, Reyanne would have agreed. She would have stood strong with an army of strangers, pointing them at danger like sharp, straight arrows and letting them fly, never intending to retrieve them. But she's done. She wants to look at tomorrow and see beyond her anger. Zanthrand—the Dark Moon of the Dominion, their leader and black magic master—has changed something in her today.

She wonders aloud, "What happens after the Dominion is defeated?"

Or the Separatists are, Zanthrand whispers into her mind, making her somehow manage to smile to herself.

You lived?

You won't be rid of me so easily, white witch.

But it doesn't come with vitriol this time. It comes out as a taunt. A tease. For a moment, Reyanne imagines affection… and then she actually feels it.

Be careful, nightmaster, or I might think you like me.

There is a long, heady pause before he responds: *What is hate if not love turned upside down?*

With that, he recedes from her mind, caught off in a dream somewhere far away.

The conversation in the room has moved on and she's no longer a part of it, which suits her just fine. Alone while with people, Reyanne plots, turning over her thoughts this way and that. Perhaps she can't convert him, but perhaps there's a way he could be hers all the same. A way that she could be his. She just has to find it.

I'm coming for you, Zanthrand.

And this time, it's not a threat. It's a promise.

You, dear reader, have earned an <u>OPEN ENDING</u>!

Remember, there are 17 possible endings, and this is just one. If you've found all nine Reyanne endings, start back at the beginning, and choose Zanthrand's path. Many diverging stories await you!

Good luck, dear reader!

CHAPTER 16

"*I* want you to go away and never return. I want to tear your face from my mind and gouge your heart from my chest. I want to be done with you now and forever." Reyanne's words come out as little, sad whispers… and she doesn't know if she means them.

She expects him to disappear now. The longer they sit here, the more their depleted stores of magic replenish. In mere seconds, Reyanne knows Zanthrand, the Dark Moon of the Dominion, will fade and escape to fight her another day. Again. And again.

"I feel the same," he admits.

She chuckles, even though it hurts. "Then find a way to break this cursed bond."

"That's not what I meant."

Zanthrand's eyes are on the ground, his body hunched over. "I don't know who I am without you. For years, my site has been set solely on you. I'm obsessed. I think about you day and night. How to thwart you, confuse you, stall you, make you speak just one more word to me. Maybe it's because I'll learn your secrets, but I'm not sure what secrets I want anymore; the Separatists',"—he looks at her more earnestly than he ever has—"…or just yours. Even when you're dreaming, you're everything. I don't know if I want to kill you, convert you…or convert myself."

It's a terrible confession. If the Dominion knew such thoughts crossed Zanthrand's mind, however fleetingly, there would be dire consequences.

Unexpected longing and vulnerability cascade through his heart in equal measures, taking Reyanne by surprise. She settles onto her hip, the one still unmarred, and stares at him until he finally looks back. Moonlight makes his pale skin seem to glow. The streaks of blood on his face look artful, as if painted with a master's brush. They suit him in their violence and agony…

Reyanne's suffering doesn't come just from her aching side. It comes from a wound drilled through her bleeding heart. A heart that beats solely for his words.

Her response is on the tip of her tongue. Everything hangs in the balance.

Dear reader, should Reyanne:

Encourage Zanthrand to join her, turn to page 84 (chapter 17)

Tell him he can never atone, turn to page 87 (chapter 18)

CHAPTER 17

"Join me," Reyanne says. It's so soft the breeze almost steals it. "If fate has bound us together—"

"*You* bound us together."

"And maybe I was meant to." She pulls herself closer, and everything about him bristles. The blood in his left eye has sealed it shut, but the one that remains fixed on her is wary. "Zan,"—she sighs his name in a way she's never allowed herself before—"it doesn't have to be this way."

He tries to chuckle, but it becomes a pained grunt. "You must think me a fool. Only death awaits me wherever you are. If you don't bring it, others will. You can't expect me to lock my hands behind my back and expose my belly to their eviscerating fingers. You can't expect me to open my ears to their insults and lies. If killing is the crime, we're all guilty... The two of us, most of all."

She flinches. Though Reyanne has fought on battlefield after battlefield, she's never applied any meaningful death toll to herself...but it's true. She's responsible for as many Separatist casualties as Dominion ones, perhaps even more now that she can't bear to destroy their greatest threat, a murderous nightmare.

"Yes," he says. "I may be a nightmare. But the Separatists are no dream, no matter how you pretend them to be. You feign innocence, but your hands are just as bloody as mine. Your armies just as ruthless. Anything for a win, Reyanne. In that, we are the same."

She wants to fight, but the will has left her. All that remains is the hollow acceptance of his words. But something warm washes over from his side of the bond.

"Yet there may be another way to end this war. A way beyond bloodshed," he muses. He's lightheaded now. Swaying. Faltering.

In the silent space between them Reyanne realizes that, despite disengaging her signal to the Dragon riders, they'll still find them soon. There's nothing but danger here. "You have to go."

He looks toward the sky, knowing their time is almost up. Though that's not entirely true. Wherever they go, there's no escaping each other.

"This conversation isn't over, white witch."

"We're connected." A small smile crosses her lips. "I suppose that means it never will be."

One of his eyebrows lifts high. "You speak as if I want this."

She *tsks* for a moment, tapping her head and then her heart. "What you know, I know."

"And what might that be?"

"You want me all for yourself."

After a haughty pause, his smile joins hers. "Perhaps. But if you're to be mine…"

Then you're mine forever, he sends into her thoughts, his yearning open to her now that the dam has broken. Their admission has changed something. It may have just changed everything. For the first time in what feels like eons, Reyanne feels hope bloom within.

She agrees. "Forever."

You, dear reader, have earned an <u>OPEN ENDING</u>!

Remember, there are 17 possible endings, and this is just one. If you've found all nine Reyanne endings, start back at the beginning, and choose Zanthrand's path. Many diverging stories await you!

Good luck, dear reader!

CHAPTER 18

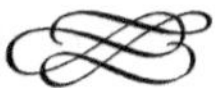

"The Separatists will never have you." It's a grim truth. One that makes his jaw clench. "You've said, done, and inspired too much evil within the Dominion. You can never atone…and the Dominion would never leave me alive, either. There's no path for us."

"Enemies, then," he agrees.

His breath shudders and she looks up to see him flagging. He seems like he's about to be sick or faint. More than that, though, his emotions are a tumultuous storm of rage and unfulfilled dreams. How could she have missed this emotion in him? Probably for the same reason she refused to see it in herself. Because it was never meant to be.

"Then let's end it," Zanthrand says. "In thirty days, meet with me. A final duel. Just us, no one else. Win or lose, I… I just need this to end."

Tears slipping over her cheeks, Reyanne nods. She may have just signed her own life away, but it is what it is. As a lonely child, Reyanne had only ever prayed to have a meaningful impact on the world. This is her moment. Live or die, she'll either cripple the Dominion or inspire the Separatists.

At her agreement, Zanthrand sighs, a deep and sad sound. His magic has replenished enough to allow him one last incantation this evening, one that makes his body become murky, yet transparent. Zanthrand is fading to black smoke, his edges blurring as his beautiful lips draw shapes against the air. In mere moments, he slips by her, leaving her bereft and alone in this soulless field of the dead.

She collapses backwards with a shuddering sob. Even as he drifts away, she feels his pain, just as he must feel hers. Still, distraction comes when she hears a voice scream "REYANNE!" from above, a dragon rider blotting out the moon. They saw her beam and found her, after all.

* * *

Queen Annora Jehanne hikes her shoulders higher, regarding Reyanne with a scrutinizing eye, hovering over her as she lies in the castle apothecary, which also serves as a medical station for mages. Though her colleague Njal Osric has healed her, Reyanne's emotions are still in need of mending. So, here she sits in the windowless room, candles throwing flickering, dim light in this place of magic and mystery.

"It's a foolish plan," Queen Annora says as her twin brother Leif mixes a draught in the background.

Once upon a time, Leif was the greatest wizard in the land, but as the Dominion rose, he fell into despair, and his power all but died. Now, it's up to Reyanne to lead the vanguard. twirling her fingers to magically raise their banners high, hovering their red insignia in the air above their enemies' heads and making them well aware of who they're standing against.

"And yet I must do it anyway," Reyanne says.

"Facing him alone is a death wish," Leif tells her, clinking bottles and measuring powders. "He'll trick you. He'll bring his people and destroy you."

"He won't." *Not without me knowing his plan,* is what Reyanne doesn't say. Her bond with Zanthrand is the most well-kept secret she has. He, too, hides the truth the way dragons hide gold. The only way people will take it from him is if they wrench off his scales one-by-one…and even then…

"You can't know that," Queen Annora says, her mouth stern. "You are the hope of the Separatists, I can't have you die over some personal battle of wills."

"If I can kill him, think of how many lives I'll save."

"If you fail, think of how many lives we'll lose," Leif counters, swirling the mixture in its flask, lifting it to the light of the high chandelier and squinting at it with one eye.

When the twins are in sync against her, Reyanne can never win. It's insulting, even though she knows it comes from a place of caring. If not about her, then about the Separatists' success.

"The Dominion is ruthless, as is the Dark Moon," Reyanne agrees. "But he fights with honor, and he is prideful. I have no doubt that he'd rather die than claim a false win over the hated White Witch."

"That's a lot of credit to give one's enemy," Annora says.

"I've divined it," Reyanne lies. "I can't see the outcome, but I know we face off alone."

Leif approaches with a sigh, handing her the calming draught that will help her sleep despite her racing mind. She needs to recoup her magic, and rest is the best remedy for that. She downs it in a single gulp, letting its bitter flavor take over her senses. Her stomach nearly rejects it, but once she wills it into submission, immediately her limbs feel heavy.

"You must allow me to do this," Reyanne says, her voice sounding far away.

"If you've seen it, child, I will trust you," Annora says.

Leif seems less inclined to believe her. Still, he nods. "You are strong Reyanne. You are his match. I will gather the others in a prayer circle to fortify—"

But the rest of the old mage's words are lost, because Reyanne is drifting far and away.

* * *

Her staff swings through the air in a quick clip as Reyanne practices her moves, hiking a leg up as she spins the elongated weapon, practicing her balance. Her muscles are so used to this, she barely needs to think about how to compensate for her shifting weight; it's all just a part of how her body now works.

An eerie, yet familiar feeling comes over her, and she takes a deep breath, settling into a defensive stance. In front of her, the world seems to warp and haze until the mirror gate opens, as it so often does. Neither she nor Zanthrand can seem to control it. Through the mirror, she cannot touch, though she can see…and see she does.

Zanthrand, too, is preparing for battle. His weapon of choice is a black sword that emits a crimson haze, glowing with a viciousness becoming a man such as him. Similar to the holy blade tucked into Reyanne's staff, Zanthrand's corrupted artifact connects to the magic all around them, and so will never dim unless he wills it.

"Are you nearing ready, white witch?"

"In five days," she nods.

"Ah. Is that how long I have to live, or you?" It comes out

with a cold smirk. One of his eyes shines a bright gold compared to his other's dark, amber brown. It's unsettling. The light comes from the eye she'd blinded in battle, though she knows through their bond it can see again, now.

Unable to help herself, she asks, "Did it hurt when you healed it?" even though she already knows the answer. Her own left eye had burned softly with his pain. A never-ending sting. It must have been so much worse for him.

"Not one bit," he lies. "But I'm grateful to you. I honed a new spell to bring it back to life. And I must admit I like the color."

"You look even more like a monster." The gold is ringed with a sickly vermillion. If both his eyes were like that, he'd look like the devil himself.

He tsks at her. "I am the devil himself. As you'll soon find out."

As he walks closer, the mirror gate approaches with him. This is not the same as the portal that sometimes puts them in the same space, so he can do her no harm here. Not with his body anyway. But with his words…

"I plan to run you through," he states simply. "Then I'll cut you from here"—his finger rests just above his navel—"to here"—and swipes up quickly, stopping just under the apex of his ribcage. "Then I'll eat your heart, Reyanne. I'll feel it beat its last in the palm of my hands before I devour it whole and raw."

The mirror comes ever nearer until she can feel the tingle of its energy. His face is so close, and his eyes are locked on hers.

"Because that's the only way I'll get to have it," Zanthrand whispers. "The only way I'll make it mine. And make no mistake…like your life, your heart belongs to me."

And with that, the mirror fades into nothing, though the longing in Zanthrand's soul taints hers with sorrow.

Indeed, it's almost time.

* * *

The dragon's wings pump, scraping against the saddle placed atop its back, without which the insides of Reyanne's thighs would be shredded on its sharp scales. As it stands, she holds the reins tightly with one hand, her staff gripped in the other.

Without it needing to be spoken aloud, Reyanne knew to carry no helm, no poisons, no rune stones. She can tell Zanthrand will be at the same disadvantage. This is a test of skill, both hand to hand, and words against words.

Reyanne has slept the last day away, ensuring she has every magical reserve at her disposal…though perhaps it was a poor decision to waste what was possibly her last day on earth.

The meager, yet nourishing meal she set in her stomach this morning weighs her down as she looks at the battleground below. He is already waiting for her there, a figure draped in black, and she begins a downward spiral on the back of her winged beast.

You could just light me aflame, he whispers into her mind.

Despite the severity of the situation, Reyanne smirks. *That would be bad form.*

Need to kill me with your own hands, then?

That ruins her smile. *I'd rather run away.* Because what's the point of hiding her feelings this late in the game?

Me, too. If I could, I'd delay this battle until the end of time.

Scared to lose, are you?

Perhaps.

The landing is rough, almost knocking the wind out of

her. Disengaging her safety clip with a snick, Reyanne hops nimbly from the Dragon's back, petting the soft scales along its throat—the only weak spot a dragon has, and one that takes the utmost trust to approach safely.

The dragon growls low, but Reyanne tut-tuts him. "It will be alright."

"Or it won't," Zanthrand adds, approaching her slowly.

"Pessimist."

"Realist," he replies.

With a last double tap, the dragon takes its cue and flaps a hard pump, disturbing the valley and making the grass waver as it soars away. Magic is always better out in the vastness of nature. Looking around, Reyanne knows this arena was the right choice.

He's behind her like doom, the heat from his body filling the space in between them. "Are you ready?"

"Will I ever be?" she asks, though the answer is no. It will always be no. "Are you sure we can't run?"

Zanthrand's head ticks back and forth slightly, his ominous eye glowing even in the sunlight. "It's too late for that."

Reyanne's eyes mist, and she wipes tears away with the back of her hand roughly, frowning like a child. Shaking her limbs out and ensuring her hair is affixed behind her, she huffs a readying breath. "Okay."

He backs away, step after step after step. "Then it's time."

The trick to fighting Zanthrand is to have multiple ideas in your head all at once—a skill she learned, oddly enough, from him. He may devise loose counters to her myriad of half-formed strikes and spells, but she can still catch him by surprise if she makes her decisions close enough to the last minute. It's a whole new way of thinking, and one in which he has her outmatched. The one true tick mark in her favor is that she beats him out in agility, his frame too large to be nimble.

He sheds his cloak, revealing his unarmored self, still and always in heavy black and brocades, but terribly informal given the pomp and circumstance they normally face each other in. It's as if she's caught him in his bedchambers, as she so often has, relaxing and reading incantations aloud under his breath, seeing what wonders they might make appear before his eyes.

Following suit, Reyanne brings two fingers to her lips and kisses them, sliding her fingerprints over the length of her staff, rooting it to the ground while she rolls her shoulders. Her heavily padded vest and arm guards fall, and she kicks them behind her, trying to look just as fearless as he does. All she senses is amusement from his side of their bond.

"Cute, am I?" She ticks her chin up at him in a challenge.

"Never," he lies once more.

And then he dives in for the kill, one she will not give him.

Her fist finds her weapon easily, grabbing it from the ground and tearing off the hidden scabbard to meet his heavy strike with her own glowing, holy blade. She manages to repel his opening move and follows up with one of her own, slashing sideways with a grunt as she uses his momentum against him. Pivoting her wrists, she re-angles the dangerous part of her staff and swipes upwards, forcing him to reel back.

"Trying to take my other eye?" he asks mildly, twirling his sword into a reverse grip.

"It *would* work in my favor."

"That, it would."

He gets up close and personal this time, spinning on his heel while his murmurs start, a dark cloud wheeling overhead as lightning calls down. Not only does Reyanne need to handle his strikes, but she needs to now avoid the white steaks raining from the sky.

She can counter his spell or continue to dodge—and dodging is something she's quite good at.

Rolling beneath a heavy swipe of his sword, she runs to a distance, weaving around shrieks from above as white flashes sear her vision.

"Unwah kadosh imagi. Unwah nocto lameir..." Reyanne whips around and points her staff at her nemesis. A beam of energy blares from the tip, drawing not only a straight line of sheer power across the air, but driving that power down to the surface beneath, tearing a chasm in the land that shakes the entire valley. Reyanne's balance-work comes in handy as the fauna beneath her feet rolls, forcing her to glance down in order to ensure that the schism isn't winding between her feet. It's a unnecessary distraction. An utter mistake.

Zanthrand leaps into the air and over the newly torn chasm, aided by his whispering words and coming at her directly from above. She barely gets her staff up in time to catch his downward swing, sparks igniting between their glowing blades. Her teeth grind as she strains under the force of his sword, his body weight overcoming her until new words fly from her mouth, blasting him with a sudden shield that throws him yards away.

He lands on his feet but slides backwards, grinning at her. "Didn't see that one coming."

"That's rare."

But he has no more banter.

His next blows are absolutely aided by magic and it's all she can do to keep up. He never relies this heavily on brute strength, and her adrenaline is taking away her ability to reason. With a hard stab forward, Reyanne's upper arm screams as if on fire, Zanthrand's blade cauterizing as it cuts. She turns away and he slashes her again, this time from behind, making two wounds that crisscross over the expanse of her skin.

Her teeth bared, she growls and lashes sideways. Going low, she aims for his groin and legs as her other hand performs gestures against her stomach, hidden from his view, though never from his mind.

With a crushing pound, the gravity around him triples, his mass hitting the earth in a rough slam as he's brought to his knees. Reyanne immediately hears the counter chant. The one that will let him fly. She hasn't mastered that yet and she needs to keep him grounded.

Coiling her calf muscles, she pushes herself into a high jump, screaming as she puts her whole strength behind a downward cut that will force him to brave the weight of the air in order to defend. His arm comes up for the most split of seconds, his eyes locked with hers…

…before he purposefully drops his blade.

Reyanne can't pull back. There's not enough time. It's happened too fast and the golden glow of her weapon swipes through the meat of his shoulder, making a diagonal line to his breastbone where it hovers, burning his clothes away.

At first there is only shock on his face. On hers. Then reality sinks in when he tries to breathe, ragged and raw and rasping, his insides ripped and burned apart.

Reyanne wrenches her blade out and throws the thing aside as if it were poison, rushing to touch his face. His hair. Anything.

She doesn't feel his pain. Why can't she feel this?

"WHY!?" she screams.

But he can't speak. He will never speak again.

Because I can't kill you, he sends, giving her his hidden thought.

"Did you plan this!?"

His eyes slip closed, and his body loosens. It's all Reyanne can do to hold him up. "Zan, please…" but there are no healing spells she knows for damage this severe. Apparently, it's a skill he's only just learned for himself. One he can't teach her…because it's too late.

"I only ever wanted to love you," she cries against his temple as she holds him.

Soul departing his body, he graces her with one last thought. One last thing to carry with her. They are the words:

So did I…

And he's gone.

Reyanne's wail echoes off the clouds, filling the valley with her anguish. It calls to her dragon, and she can hear his wings pumping ever closer, but she doesn't want to leave this place. She wants to stay forever, living out a fantasy in her own mind. One where she held him alive and whole. One where they met as children and gave each other the love they never had growing up. One where they escaped the war and ran away together. One where they ran away tonight.

But, again, it's too late.

And it always will be.

You, dear reader, have earned a <u>SAD ENDING</u>!

Remember, there are 17 possible endings, and this is just one. If you've found all nine Reyanne endings, start back at the beginning, and choose Zanthrand's path. Many diverging stories await you!

Good luck, dear reader!

Zanthrand's nemesis lifts her mage's staff, and aims a golden beam of light toward the sky. She's calling her blasted dragon riders. If they arrive, not only will they save her, but they'll kill him, of that Zanth has no doubt.

He's too weak in his current state to do anything but submit. Being ripped apart by dragons isn't exactly how he imagined his untimely demise, though he supposes there are worse ways to go, like getting dragged away for public execution by the white witch's underlings.

The thought is sobering. It's not the pain of death Zanth is afraid of. It's the humiliation.

Reyanne of the White clutches her side with soiled fingers, leaving dark stains on her clothes before going to her knees again. Zanth's body screams with her pain as well as his own, their connection forever cursing him. Moreover, the eye she raked her magic across is dimming. Not just seeing the bright red of his own blood. Seeing nothing.

"Too weak to handle your own weapon, Reyanne? You'd let others bring me to die?"

"You *should* die," she growls, glaring at him from mere yards away.

"Perhaps," he says, body sagging. "Or perhaps you should leave me behind to suffer. These wounds will kill me soon enough. That way you, the mighty warrior for morality, need not stain your hands." Zanth looks at the corpse-littered ground with a smirk. "Though, I suppose it's too late for that."

Panting, she bares her teeth at him, pressing her palm to her side to staunch the bleeding.

"You're infecting it," he says.

"Like you care," she bites back.

He does, like it or not. He's nothing without her to rail against and he knows it. His whole life is built around defeating her and the strength she brings to the Separatists. She may be his enemy, but she is also his obsession. Men thrilled by the hunt don't do well when you take their quarry away. If your prize goes extinct, what's the point anymore?

Reyanne is the last of her kind. No one else could stand

against Zanthrand, the mighty Dark Moon of the Dominion. How very boring life would become without her. Not only that, but in his most secret of hearts, he knows he harbors specific *feelings* for her. Ones he refuses to admit.

Instead, he shakes his head slightly. "I care for nothing and no one. Definitely not a woman like you."

It hurts her somehow. Hearing those words sends a twinge through Zanth's heart that does not belong to him.

"You're lying," she says in a whisper, her body quaking as her staff glows upward, bringing his doom down upon him.

"You think I'd bother deceiving you now?"

Yes. He most definitely would.

"Why aren't you trying to run?" she asks.

"I'm not afraid of death. Don't you want to watch me fall to your friends and comrades? To watch my life's blood drain away? To make a mockery of everything I've built for myself by parading me like a fool to my own execution?"

She hangs her head, breathing deeply. He can see the conflict on her face just as much as he can feel it roiling in her heart; she's unsure of what to do with him.

Looking up, she comes to some sort of decision. "No one can kill you but me."

Her flare of possessiveness is not lost on him. He understands that feeling quite well.

After a heady pause of just connecting eyes with her, he says, "So do it. Let me die with valor on the battlefield."

Tears seep from her eyes, incongruent with her violence. Perhaps she just needs her fires stoked.

"After all," Zanth says, "You've murdered so many. What's one more?"

"I do it for righteousness. To save lives."

"Come, come now, Reyanne. Look around you. How many have you saved today?"

Casting her eyes over the canyon of the dead, Reyanne

bends over at the waist, and Zanth feels her bile rise. Instead of riling her up, he's cowing her. That disappoints him in a way he can't describe. He likes it when she fights him. If she submits, it's to be under entirely different circumstances. Soft and sweet ones.

He cuts off that line of thought immediately.

She inhales loudly through her nose, and he knows she's trying to replenish her stores of magic. He'll let her. Perhaps that will make his death quick. There's very little time to goad her now. It's only moments until the Separatists' beasts descend from the sky.

A far-off screech proves him right, and Reyanne's eyes rocket toward the sound with a grimace. He catches her thoughts clearly.

I'm going to regret this.

He silently tells her, *No matter your choice, you're absolutely right.*

She chuckles, her timbre dry and defeated, before raising her free arm in his direction, two fingers pointing toward Zanth's face. He closes his eyes to let her magic take his life, and her words echo across the high ridges of canyon stone.

"Iyath hannana, koti korosh."

Zanth is stunned. He knows that spell. Opening his eyes, he finds her gazing in his direction, but not directly at him. A sense of self-satisfaction rolls through their bond.

She's made him dim.

Invisible.

Like this, the Separatists will never find him.

"Live to fight another day, Zanthrand," she says under her rapid breath. "It's you and I in the end. Your life is mine."

Again, he feels that possessive flare. It ignites something within him. He mirrors the feeling back to her, and her smile widens for a moment before she faints to the ground, her last stunt having drained her completely.

Another dragon screams out, closer this time, and Zanth can hear heavy wings pumping, the dull flaps only moments away. He looks up to see talons scraping through the cloud cover before the rest of the dragon sinks into view, white scales picking up the shine of the moon, reflecting it like twinkling stars. Red marks leave trails like bloody finger smears over the creature's pale wings. It's powerful. Large. Deadly.

"REYANNE!" the dragon rider screams. A soon-to-be dead man on a beast's back. Zanth moves his lips to chant a spell…but no sound comes out.

The witch has taken his voice.

Clever. She'd hid her hand gestures once his eyes had closed, casting a silent spell alongside the one she spoke aloud. No wonder she'd fainted. He should have seen that coming.

The dragon lands heavily, kicking up dust and rocks at the far end of Reyanne's body, and thank the Gods for that. There's no glory in being trampled to death under a Separatist's mythical monster.

"Reyanne!" the man calls again and again, flipping her over and checking her wounds in a way that feels far too intimate. Zanthrand's teeth clench as he tries to rise, but what could he do now?

He focuses on his temper, willing it not to boil over as the unknown bastard picks up Zanth's prize. The man rests Reyanne on his lap atop the dragon's saddle, moving her this way and that to ensure she won't be cut on the thing's razor scales. Sniffing the air, the dragon looks straight at Zanth, seeing through the magic ward, but it must count him among the dead, as it does nothing. Instead, it flexes its powerful back legs after its master clucks and jumps with a heavy grace, catching itself on the wind and carrying Reyanne the

White—the hope of the Separatists, Zanth's enemy and his everything—far, far and away.

* * *

Zanth opens his eyes—well, his one eye. He's mostly nude, covered in medicinal salves as he rests in a firelit room. Only a thin blanket over his hips protects Zanth's nakedness from the eyes of others, though he doesn't care either way. If they're to be jealous of him for his throne, let them be jealous of him for everything.

His knights stand around him, coated in charcoal black and heavy armor, making them look all the more terrifying for it.

"Master," Kentat says, dropping to one knee. "We've done our best to treat you, but your eye—"

"Is beyond your capabilities," Zanth murmurs, already knowing. "It doesn't matter. My magic will save it once I've rebuilt my stores."

Magic is like that. Though there is an unlimited amount flowing through the universe, every sorcerer is simply a cup to fill. The power itself may be endless, but when your coffers are dry, they're dry. Only time and rest will do the trick and set you to rights again.

Thank the Gods Zanth is the strongest warrior in the land. It keeps him alive in battle even when his spells have given out, as they often do. Zanth prides himself in wringing out every last one before falling back on the more mundane tactics of war, though. There's more artistry in weaving words than bluntly clobbering anything within reach.

Yan speaks up. "Who did this to you, master?"

What a deceptive question. Zanth has to catch himself

before he lets out a sardonic laugh. To the untrained eye, the knight seems as if he would exact revenge on Zanth's behalf, but the more likely truth is that the man is still digging for who to betray his master to. Even after all this time, Yan is looking for someone, anyone, to finish Zanth off. It would allow the knight a chance to finally battle for a place on the Dominion's jagged throne of onyx and honor. After all, bloodlines don't matter here. Only strength.

Zanth refuses to give any names.

Especially not hers.

"War did this to me," he says. "Our troops had all fallen long before the battle was done. Yet, here I stand, having taken down as many as you could only dream. Are you going to challenge me in my time of weakness, Yan? Is that the honorable win that will earn you glory? Or will it make you a coward in the eyes of my people?"

There is no worse sin than being a coward, which is the only reason Zanthrand is still alive right now, as sure as the sunset.

Yan joins Kentat on his knees. "I would never think of betraying you, Master."

"Lies," Zanth says. "But it matters not. Come at me when it counts, and I'll be sure to defeat you in the most visceral of ways. For now, though, if you'd like to keep your insides *inside you,* I recommend taking your leave. All of you, take your leave."

With murmurs of agreement and varying amounts of loyalty, they do.

Zanth's chest fills with air, belly to breast, before it puffs out again. Everything aches. He's exhausted. Still, the white witch tickles in his mind, so he checks in on her. Seeing from behind her eyes, she's receiving similar treatment within the Separatists' castle walls. He hears the echoes of her conversation and listens in for a few moments before her annoyance at his obvious intrusion bleeds over.

Careful, Reyanne. You know I can hear everything they say. Shall I find out all the plots against me through your ears?

And with that, she pulls into silence, likely after taking a sleeping draught.

Zanth enjoys keeping her isolated from her leadership. It keeps her focused on him—something he likes very much. Whether killing her, dying by her hand, or taking her for himself, he wants her eyes ever on him.

He can only think these sinful thoughts when she's sleeping. It's one of the reasons dreamland escapes him. He'd rather stay up late imagining all the ways she can be his. His victim, his death song, his lover. His queen.

"Why did you let me live?" he wonders aloud. There are so many reasons she could have chosen within the myriad of half-formed possibilities that float around the white witch's head. But which one is most likely?

Dear reader, does Zanth think:

Reyanne felt pity for him, turn to page 106 (chapter 20)

Reyanne was afraid to make the killing blow, turn to page 112 (chapter 21)

CHAPTER 20

$\mathcal{P}$ity. That's the only word that rings true. Zanth's lips pull down at the corners and the stretch makes his face throb. Not only did she half blind him, but a painful gash winds its way from his forehead to his cheek, disfiguring him. Not that it matters. He's never been a beauty, anyway.

Seeing him prostrate before her must have seemed like a gainless win, just like it would have been for his knights. There's no true victory in taking advantage of an opponent who is weakened. One must take them out at the peak of their vitality. Run them through. Remove their heads. Stop their heart with a softly spoken spell. That's the only way to truly conquer your enemy.

So, yes, the white witch had taken pity on him. The very thought stirs a slow burn of anger. His muscles tense and twitch with energy that longs to be released.

It's then that all sound seeps away. Zanth grits his teeth, smelling a scent like fresh snow, yet feeling no cold.

The mirror gate has opened.

He doesn't know how he feels about this aspect of their

bond. A mist of what looks like night stars frames an oval window of sorts, letting him see through the miles to find his soul-bound sinner. Reyanne lies unconscious on her bed… which may as well be the other half of his bed for how close she is. He's near enough to hear her breathe.

He runs his fingertips over the electric static of the mirror gate's surface, unable to break through and touch her like he can when the portal rips open and puts them in each other's space—another unfortunate possibility of their connection. Instead, he watches the hairs on his arm stand up, the skin thrumming and prickling, causing another dull ache under all his other pains.

"I'll kill you, Reyanne. I promise."

Turning onto his side with a soft groan, he stares at her with his one remaining eye. She's on her back, her arms draped up and over the pillow beneath her head, her beating heart completely defenseless. He'd eat it if he could. Or perhaps he'd just caress her breastbone, stroking down the valley between her soft mounds. He imagines she'd make the most enthralling little sighs.

"If I don't kill you, I swear to the Gods, I'll make you mine. I'll take your mouth and your body. Your heart and your soul. I'll take your womb and your future. Everything about you will exist only for me."

She murmurs then, blinking awake slowly. Zanth tucks his need away and focuses again on his anger. Her eyes touch his, her focus fading in and out, the draught doing its job and keeping her on the thin edge of sleep.

"Fight me," Zanth whispers, though, to his ears, it comes out like a lover. As if he said, "Be with me" or "Stay with me" or even "I love you." Words that will never grace his lips.

Of all things, her mouth curls up at the corners, making her look playful. "Now?"

How adorable she is in this moment, half-gone and half-there.

"Soon," he says. "A rematch."

Her eyelids flutter closed again, and she nuzzles into her downy bed, curling into a ball. "Mm. T'morrow."

He smiles at her. He can't help it. "No. We must be at our strongest, my white witch."

"Not yours," she snuffles, then drifts back down into oblivion.

Zanth's fingers caress the surface of the mirror gate once more. "Yes, you are."

* * *

He had given her time to heal. That's all he would offer. After that, he'd called her to their favorite dueling spot—at least, the one they've fought in most often. This stretch of skrag grass and dust is a halfway point between the first Dominion outpost and the last Separatist one—a no man's land, so to speak. Here, far away from the towns and villages and other prying eyes, Zanth and his white witch can fight to their heart's content. And that's exactly what Zanth intends to do.

Rotating his wrist in a flourish, he revels in his deep affinity for his weapon, a black hilted broadsword with a crimson, flickering aura that looks like hellfire. Reyanne counters its might with a white staff sporting a glowing blade on the end, normally housed within an enchanted scabbard.

His opponent's downswing is like a scythe as she splits the air, coming far too close to his new, magical eye. One that glows. Through it, he can see her in an ultra-real way. The heat at her pulse points seems to radiate a haze of a color he can't define. Her eyes have gone from dark olive to blinding lime-green shimmers and it's all he can do not to be hypnotized by the sight of her.

Her blade shears off a bit of his ragged cape as he backs away from her attack, twirling a counter strike with both hands on his weapon, ensuring a heavy hit that her frail arms will have trouble holding back.

"Ek-*kratza!*" Zanth says through his teeth, and Reyanne's knees go loose, ensuring he gets a good swipe at the meat of her hip before she can dodge him with a counter spell. Her guttural cry should please him, but it doesn't.

Even knocked to the ground, her eyes scream violence as her free hand lifts and draws a circle in the air. Along the path of her stroke, characters light up in white, branding Zanth's eyes with their bright flashes. Druid magic. Rune-stone writing. He barely has moments.

Like lightning, they crackle toward him as he tries to twist away to no avail. Several spiking letters slam into his torso, penetrating his clothes and leaving glowing writing on his skin before sending a sizzle that electrifies his nerves, making his whole body rigid as he grunts.

His incapacitation gives the white witch a chance to heal herself; he can see the chant and choreography form in her mind—but not today. Zanth bites his lip and spits his blood at her. Immediately, the spatter elongates into something like an oil slick, whipping up and latching onto her wrists, dragging her to the ground to be wrapped up in his pain. The wards she had cast fade, and Zanth's trembling body comes back to itself in time to see her panicked expression as she struggles.

He could end her now—they've been at this for hours—but he hesitates.

Her muffled scream pummels the slick that covers her

mouth, melting it away with her sheer volume, like a banshee cry. Zanth is forced to cover his ears as his mind whites out in sync with the budding crest of dawn.

Sensing her intention, he growls, "Don't you *dare!*"

But it doesn't matter. Wounded, Reyanne's free lips chant her familiar spell as the daylight touches her face, and her body blazes with radiance. He can't touch her like this. She's like the sun.

Transcendent, her head tips back, white rays burning Zanth's eyes. When he peeks between cupped fingers, Reyanne has pulled her dirty trick again, turning into an orb of light and floating in the air out of range.

"WITCH!" he screams. "THIS ISN'T OVER!"

Reyanne whispers into his mind, *It is for today.*

Zanth's hand goes to his hip, feeling the searing wound he'd given her as if it were on his own body. It leaves an ache the way her absence does. "Cunning bitch." He swipes the back of his hand over his bitten lip, already swelling, and watches her go.

She's going to drive him insane.

* * *

The mirror gate opens again that night, and Reyanne is hunched over herself, back to him, trembling. She doesn't notice him and Zanth knows why. His black oil seeped poison into her. It was supposed to bring her crashing down, weakening her until he could spirit her away, yet here she sits in her own castle room, colorful and bright.

Zanth takes her in. She's naked. It's not the first time he's caught her like this, though it's the first time he's had a moment to truly appreciate it. She's too thin, as if the Separatists refuse to feed her. Her ribs line her sides in ridges and valleys, and her vertebrae knot her back inch after inch. He wouldn't let that happen. If she were caught in his snare, he'd feed her until she was round with his generosity. Maybe in more than one way, filled with his seed.

It's that lustful spike that turns her over her shoulder toward him, one arm going to the curve of her breasts in defense while her knees press so hard together, they quake. The wound on her hip oozes with terrible blackness that crawls up her veins in dark spiderwebs.

"Are you suffering?" he asks, almost amused by the question.

"Not as bad as you did when I took your eye," she says, feisty as ever, though her face is blotchy and coated with the tell-tale tracks of tears.

"And yet I have it back again." He gestures at his winding scar and glowing orb, making her look away. He doesn't feel revulsion from her side of their bond, but a deep-seated guilt. He almost hears the apology that forms on the tip of her tongue, but a flare of agony pulses through her wound once more, the words becoming a whimper of pain. Her hands grip into tight fists even as she blocks her prone body from his prying eyes.

Seeing her this way fills Zanth with emotion.

Dear reader, does Zanth feel:
Sympathy, turn to page 115 (chapter 22)
Righteous and proud, turn to page 118 (chapter 23)

CHAPTER 21

She was afraid. That must be it. If their bond connects them in their pain, what will happen if one of them dies? Will the other follow into oblivion, or will the bond break? Zanth supposes he'll only know once it's too late to change his mind.

Still, this is a weakness to exploit. She has an obvious soft spot for him—not that the feeling isn't mutual. For as much as they hiss at each other, they both know there's something hidden underneath the animosity. It's as if they try even harder to stay in their respective, war-addled corners if only to deny the consequences of the soul-bond she has wrought. The bond that ended their eternal loneliness.

What if he were to turn the tides? She created the bond to bring him to the light; what if Zanth could perform the same sort of trickery, but on an emotional level instead of a spiritual one? And not to convert, but to overcome? His feelings aside, an enemy is an enemy and must be destroyed.

This would indeed take some heavy lifting on his part. Disguising his intentions from her may be near impossible. He can't tell outright lies; she'll see right through him. But he often gets away with half-truths. She's too stubborn to dive too deeply into his mind, some misplaced sense of righteousness. Thankfully, he doesn't share the same scruples. He's dug into her every nook and cranny and soaked it up like bread soaks up wine.

Reyanne was abandoned as a child. That's why the idea of their soul-bond came to her in the first place. She must have wagered that if she could bring her equal in magic to her side of the war, not only would winning be assured, but she'd have someone who understood her. Understood the pain of being *other*. The sorrow of no one truly knowing you. Oh, but he knows her. Down to her dark corners.

What if I told her that her mercy meant something to me?

Because it did, just not in the way she might think.

What if I told her that I wanted to talk—not just through our bond, but in a way where we can't be torn from one another...?

Their bond brings many mysteries into existence. One of which is something they call the "mirror gate". Like a glass pane on the wall, ornate in its star-swirling frame, the mirror lets them view each other, as through a window, though they cannot touch. Other times, however, their connection becomes a powerful portal, a strange shift in space that puts them in the same location. Then they can *absolutely* touch. And touch they do—weapon to weapon, spell to spell. But it's unpredictable, fickle, closing before either of them can strike a killing blow.

Neither their mind connection, the mirror gate, nor the physical portal would be enough for him to coax her sentiments in his favor. If they were truly in the same location, however, he could tell her she's changed him. Another half-truth. Though she has certainly changed the way he interacts with another human being—her, specifically—she has not changed his heart. Not in any way he's willing to face.

Still, there would be enough honesty in this plan to let his feelings and his mind read true, should she care to skim the surface of his thoughts. Her guard will lower then. Her will to fight will lessen. That's when he'll be able to kill her.

He should trick her immediately. The faster, the better, so he doesn't have a chance to give himself away. Yet, move too soon and she may not trust his requests for a peaceful conversation.

What to do?

DEAR READER, does Zanth:

Play the long game, turn to page 133 (chapter 26)
Trick her now, turn to page 170 (chapter 27)

CHAPTER 22

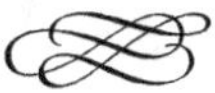

Sympathy makes him press his lips together, dropping his gaze from her current frailty. She wouldn't want him to see her like this and that matters, somehow.

"It doesn't have to be this way, Reyanne. You and I."

Her laugh is grim. "And what should it be, then? You want me to join you, to become a cruel, dark magician? Or will you finally convert yourself to the ways of the light?"

"Why must it be a pendulum? Does one have to swing from one apex to the other? Don't pretend we are pure, Reyanne. Though you focus on white magic, that doesn't preclude you from dabbling in the dark, just as I dabble in white."

"Yet we both know exactly where our strengths, and our allegiances, lie."

Zanth stares at the floor, his cold marble looking back at him with its wavering lines of white streaked throughout its dark surface. It's so like him.

"I'm tired of the war between our two ideologies," he says. "Tired of fighting. Tired of the sorrow it brings my people.

Never mind submitting; if you would simply stand down, we could find a way toward peace."

It's an idea that falls from his lips without him thinking. He's not sure his people will abide by such a thing, given the pain the Separatists have caused them, but Zanthrand the Dark Moon brokers no room for argument. If he chooses not to let any more soldiers die, then, by the Gods, that's exactly what will happen.

"It will never work," Reyanne says through an intake of breath, rubbing an elixir into her open wound. If she seals it like that, she'll never extract the poison. She needs to either counteract it first or have someone suck the venom from her. He'd do it. He would fly to her side in moments if she'd only ask. Over his dead body would anyone else put their lips on her.

She continues, "It's more than just defending our own territories and you know it. The Separatists fight against your oppressive regime. The Dominion inflicts only terror in the hearts of its people."

"Terror breeds compliance, Reyanne."

"Or rebellion."

He hates that word. He hates the concept. He hates this conversation. Partially because she's right. He's a hair's breadth away from being betrayed at any time by his own monsters in human skin, his knights a threat every day they live and breathe. Not to mention his war council. His Lords. Anyone who covets his throne, no matter how silently, is a danger to him. The thought of an uprising of his people, though—that's both terrible and terrifying.

"That's why I must be strong," he says. "I'll quell any dissent with an iron fist and blood-stained fingers, if that's what it takes."

"You're a fool," she tells him. She means it without

offense. Still, a thread of insecurity winds its way around Zanth's heart.

DEAR READER, **does Zanth:**

Double down, turn to page 123 (chapter 24)

Consider her point of view more seriously, go to page 126 (chapter 25)

CHAPTER 23

"You brought this on yourself," Zanth tells her.

She turns away and bends at the waist, taking more medicine and gently pressing it against her wound. It's not helping. Those black poison lines are working their way up her side enough to make him worry.

He growls. "If you would just submit, this could all be over. Instead, you're a fool who does nothing but cause pain. To your comrades. Your people. Yourself. Is that the part you want to play in this life? If so, no wonder your parents left you."

With a gasp, she whips around, still shielding her body but with hurt obvious on her face. Zanth has seen her memories down to the very last haze of childish whimsy; he knows how deeply her abandonment and loneliness have ruined her.

Her expression pulls into a sneer. "As a man so ruthless his own family tried to kill him, who are you to talk? My parents may have considered me a burden, but yours knew you were a monster!"

Now it's his turn to hurt. Their deepest wounds are always laid bare to each other. He hates it.

He clasps his hands into fists tight enough to make his bones creak and glares at her with one iris of brown and another of sickly gold. They pause for a moment, feeding their anger and indignancy back and forth in a never-ending loop…until Reyanne's eyelids flutter. Zanth can feel light-headedness take her over. She's flagging.

It's the poison.

"What are you treating that with?"

She presses her lips together, stubborn, so he dips into her mind, taking what he needs from the twists of pink matter that house her thoughts.

Shaking his head, a small tick side to side, he says, "No. That's not right. That will only make the venom spread faster."

A deep worry seeps into them both.

"I don't know what this is," she says, gesturing at her wound through heavy sniffles, eyes watering with pain. "I don't know how to treat it!"

"Go to your apothecary! Certainly, your mages—"

"Have all gone to fortify our wards and shields. I'm alone!"

And his heart is in this throat. Pressing his palms over the mirror gate, he panics. "Get dressed. Go where your stores are. I can tell you the ingredients for the antidote!"

Giving up her modesty, she tries to stand…and drops. He has no mind for the shape of her now. Instead, he pounds against the clear barrier that keeps them apart. "Reyanne, if you don't reach your elixirs, you will die. Get up."

"Zan…" she tries as she lifts onto her hands, her entire side a pattern of black threads that now run up through her shoulder and down her arm. It's only minutes until it gets to her heart.

"No," he says. "No. You don't get to die like this!"

With a pathetic laugh, she asks, "Did-didn't you want to kill me?"

"I wanted to *weaken* you! To *trap* you! I was going to bring you back with me!"

"As a prisoner?" she manages through a crackling throat.

"It doesn't matter! You would have just been mine!"

A scoff comes. Her arms are trembling as she tries to hold herself up. "W-we're quite a pair, you and I."

"Hold on." Zanth says. "I'll come to you. I'll—"

"—Be too late," she finishes, panting now. Everything is moving so much faster. He can actually see the lines bleed across her body, eerie and horrifying.

This will not be how she leaves this world; Zanth refuses it. With a grunt, he digs his nails into the mirror gate, turning its crackling static into flickers of lightning that glide over his fingertips. He's going to open the portal. He has no idea if he can do it, but *goddamn it,* he's going to try.

Tears, he pushes into her mind. *If you can't get to your herbs, you must use tears of sorrow!*

But she's not answering.

He bellows then. It gets him nowhere, so he changes tactics, his voice falling into a murmur of words, using the lightest magic he knows. If the mirror gate won't open, he'll rip his own portal through existence. It's been years since he's used the sacred skills of the white mages, but his pride be damned, he'll use every spell in his arsenal.

"E'tua. E'tash. Ik'not'e. Ifriith."

There is a sound like thunder that booms so hard it pummels his chest. This is not like the portal their bond creates, setting them in each other's spaces; this is a hole in reality, and Zanth will be the one who shreds his way through the veil.

More words fall from him, so quiet they're lost in the

rumbling air, though the magic hears him anyway. That's all that matters.

This is all taking too long, and he tries to keep his panic at bay, but it's crawling up his throat like a monster set on devouring his mind.

With a horrible rending crack, the portal finally opens like a gash in the air—a rip of uneven, jagged edges, looking as if they could slice anything that touches them. Not that it would stop him. Sweating with fear and his blood roaring, Zanth slides to his knees before his obsession, turning her over in his arms. She is both hard and soft at the same time, her bones and muscle making her lean while her femininity keeps her plush.

"Please, Reyanne," he begs, watching her closed eyes and her labored breath. His entreaties bring tears to his eyes, and he catches them, pressing them to her side in soft drips, but it's too little, too late. No matter how he weeps, no matter how he sobs, she's already gone.

Or is she?

Zanth is holding her hand to his face as his sorrow rolls in droplets over the curve of her palm, and he feels...a twitch.

Pulling back, he can see her lips part as her brows knit.

"That's it, princess. You can do it."

He caresses the jut of her hip with his wet fingers and watches the black marks on her arm recede.

"Wh—?" she tries, and he shushes her.

"The tears neutralize the poison."

"Ex-extract?"

"No need." He shakes his head. "Shh. I've got you."

"How did you—?"

"Get here?" he completes her thought. "Simple. All I had to do was tear the world apart."

And, wonder of wonders, she smiles. Eyes still closed, cradled in his arms, she asks, "What happens now?"

"Don't worry about anything but this moment." He dares to press a kiss on her forehead as he pulls her into an embrace, rocking her healing body. "Tomorrow will bring what it brings. Our fates and futures await, I promise you. But tonight, please…just let me hold you."

She nuzzles against his chest as she relaxes into his arms. Her face holds no fear, nor anger; only trust and softness. For the very first time since he's known her, Reyanne of the White submits to his will.

And that's when Zanthrand falls in love.

You, dear reader, have earned an <u>OPEN</u> <u>ENDING</u>!

Remember, there are 17 possible endings, and this is just one. If you've found all eight Zanthrand endings, start back at the beginning, and choose Reyanne's path. Many diverging stories await you!

Good luck, dear reader!

CHAPTER 24

His ominous eye glows as he stares at her, no longer caring about her vulnerability. Zanthrand lives to take advantage of such weaknesses. He doubles down on his way of life. "Did you ever notice that in my inner territories, life is good? It's only my cities and soldiers that suffer. But no. You close your eyes to any of my success and focus on failures that you, yourself, bring to my people."

She scoffs, but he's having none of it.

"The Separatists *disgust* me," he continues. "Hypocritical filth. Did you know your farmers are forced to fight, Reyanne? There is no one you won't conscript. You send the untrained to the slaughter regardless of the fact that my militant nation easily destroys your endless horde of the frail."

She looks at him with wide eyes. "I…"

"Ah. Never privy to the machinations of your superiors, are you?"

"Because you keep me isolated! Because I can't let them know we're connected! How could you know such a thing, anyway?!"

Zanth hides the identity of his spy deep in his mind. He holds the woman's sister hostage in order to garner compliance. Cruelty does, indeed, have its place.

"Does it matter?" he asks. "The truth remains. And, make no mistake, we'll kill anyone you throw at us."

"I hate you! I will bring down everything you stand for!" she yells. Through their bond, he feels her vitriol...and loathes it.

He narrows his eyes. "And that is why you must die. Why you *will* die. You want to be the one who ends me, Reyanne? I wish you good luck. You will be taken down long before I am."

And he means it this time. If he can be rejected, if he must feel her hatred for him in his heart, then let him return it tenfold.

He touches the mirror gate. "I hope my poison takes you. I no longer care how your life's candle snuffs out—by my hand, a firebomb, a mutiny. Die, Reyanne. Only then will my country know peace."

His words hurt her even through her hostility, and for that, he is glad.

"Time will tell, Zanthrand," she says, hard and soft at the same time.

"Yes," he agrees, refusing to waver regardless of how his heart tries to rebel against him. "And with your numbers dwindling, time is ever on my side."

With that, the mirror gate closes and Zanth is left in regret, needing to consider what comes now. Does he truly wish her dead? Yes and no. It's always been both. Though it seems he must choose one over the other, after all...

You, dear reader, have earned an <u>OPEN ENDING</u>!

Remember, there are 17 possible endings, and this is just one. If you've found all eight Zanthrand endings, start back at the beginning, and choose Reyanne's path. Many diverging stories await you!

Good luck, dear reader!

CHAPTER 25

"Perhaps. But only because I dream of a time when I won't have to be the God that punishes his sinners," Zanth admits. "I dream of…more."

Still covering her bare chest and wincing from her medicinal treatment, she turns toward him. "The Separatists have 'more'. Everyone deserves the right not to have oppression breathe its foul breath over everything they do. They can choose how to live their lives."

"Choose dissension, you mean. Without oversight, all anyone would see is conflict after conflict, differences in opinion and ideas becoming seeds for chaos and violence. The self-righteous will win attention for their half-thought-out points of view and spend lifetimes pushing their own vain agendas."

Reyanne smiles ever so slightly. "And isn't that amazing?"

Zanth's eyebrows knit.

"How far can you get with only one voice of truth coming down from on high?" she asks. "How can one person know every possible path toward success? How can one mind understand the needs of all? Only by giving the people voices, letting them have passion for what they believe in, can we thrive. Your people have differing ideas, too. You just kill them in cruel ways and allow no opportunity for growth and change.

"But what happens after you die, Zanthrand?" she continues. "You believe your actions righteous, but can you claim that anyone who succeeds you will continue your legacy? That they'll adopt your ideology? Or is there a chance they could topple your kingdom and end your people? Is that the *'more'* you seek?"

Zanth's heart is in a vise. He trusts absolutely no one to care about his people the way that he does. He may be a hammer that pounds the subversive nail from time to time, but those who would vie for his throne would only act as a manic fist, indiscriminately crushing all.

Reyanne continues, "We envision a world where the best of the best ideas can come to the forefront. Where the desires of the people can take precedence over the will of a single sovereign."

"Yet you boast the legacy blood-reign of an aged queen. You can't be that naïve," Zanth says. "Despite her pretty words, your sovereign's need for power would crush any who would seize it for themselves. She would silence them and spout their beliefs as her own just to stay at the top."

"Maybe. But I have faith. I believe that she can create a better future *together* with the people. That's where you and I differ. That's why we can never come together on the same side. It's about more than just light magic versus dark, the Separatists versus the Dominion. It's about believing in others to do the right thing. You, Zan, you only ever believe in yourself."

He flinches at how right her words are, the sting of them like a slap across his face.

With that, the mirror gate closes.

He takes a deep breath to center himself. Reyanne is sharp sometimes, both with her words and her wit, seeing beyond what's said aloud to the truth of things hiding behind embellished facades. That may give her some special insight into the ways of the world Zanth can't divine for himself.

However, something the white witch doesn't know—something *no one* really knows—is that her beloved Separatist Queen is Zanthrand's own mother. It's a part of the Dark Moon's puzzle Reyanne has never put together. Long ago, Zanth had been a prince named Brahm, a young man who had sought only to deserve the heavy burden of the crown. His mother was a harsh mentor. Unforgiving. Unwavering. She demanded the best of him with no leniency, working him to the core until he'd achieved great rank and respect beneath her. With his dedication to scholarship, fearlessness and valor, he even attainted the rare, honored title of Sorcerer Knight just as he turned to his twentieth year…and that was when his uncle Leif, his first and dearest mentor, tried to kill him.

Poison.

A coward's attack.

Zanth had always assumed his mother was the mastermind behind everything. The royals made a grand announcement that it was his uncle Seth, an exiled, dark magic master, who took Brahm's life as a part of some imaginary plot—treacherous lies to fill the ears of the lower class, distracting them from finding out that the true criminal sat on their own throne. Zanth knew in his gut that his mother was afraid of his budding prowess, unwilling to pass the torch of leadership. If young prince Brahm in all his excellence had stayed at the castle, he would have taken a bite of the feast she hoarded for herself.

But what if Zanth was wrong? For Reyanne to believe in her Queen so deeply, she must see a side of his mother that

Zanth never had. Never could. He was too busy being afraid to fail.

When Brahm escaped death and found his way to his exiled uncle, the only one who could hide him, his mother had made her kingdom mourn the picture-perfect prince they'd lost. Zanth hated the way she garnered attention and sympathy for a son she ordered to die…but what if it wasn't her order at all? What Leif had acted alone in his betrayal? What if the queen truly wept when her only child was supposedly destroyed? What if his mother was indeed a hard woman, but one who had nevertheless loved him underneath her crystalline edges? What would she do if she knew her little Brahm was still alive today?

Something twists inside him, unbidden tears forming in his eyes.

If Queen Jehanne is truly a good woman and her ideals are not just words, then what is he doing? If what Reyanne said is real, the Separatists stand a chance to truly flourish on their own and Zanth is simply a magic monster with a grudge, turning a blind eye to peace.

But the Dominion will never give the Separatists that; not so long as they stand. The Dark Moon may be able to steer his ship over stormy seas, but he can't change the ocean tides. The war will only end with his mother's absolute destruction.

Unless…

"Ergol," he says, and an owl with the most beautiful, tawny markings appears from nowhere, landing upon his raised forearm with elegant grace. Swiping his fingers over his eyelashes, Zanth captures his tears and conjures a vial to hold them. "Bring this to Reyanne of the White. It is the antidote to her poison." He tips his head to the side and considers. "Then return. I'll have one more thing for you to give to her. And you must not fail."

The stunning creature runs its beak over Zanth's hand in adoration as he tucks the vial into a satchel wrapped around the bird's neck.

"Fly far and fly fast, little one. She needs you."

Just like she needs what he's about to do next.

* * *

Done, Zanth thinks to himself, even as Reyanne pounds against his mental walls. Still, as much as she doesn't want this, she does. Part of it, anyway.

Zanth's loyal owl wheels through the dark sky, carrying scrolls that contain all the weaknesses of the Dominion. Maps to their unguarded nooks and crannies. Passphrases to get through the locked gates that protect their weapons caches and food stores. Entire lists of Dominion citizens who Zanth knows are looking to subvert the system from the inside—ones he's been watching for years to see if he can tease out any further plots—will all now contactable by the Separatists. By Reyanne. By his mother.

More than that, Zanth found simple transgressions or planted false evidence that would merit executing the more ruthless of his knights, a task he took quite some enjoyment in. He has publicly declared the right of succession to General Alec Schezain—a bloodthirsty cur, but a tactical idiot. The Separatists will find it easy to guess his game and strategize around him...especially since Zanth hypnotized the man and stole his battle plans in advance. Those jewels of knowledge are also winging off into the night towards Zanth's once-enemies.

This is what he can do. This is all he can do.

STOP! Reyanne screams in his mind. *NOT LIKE THIS!*

My people need this war to end. I'm willing to make the outcome tip in your favor, even if it comes at a personal cost. Why deny a gift laid down at your feet?

His eyes mist as he looks off into the nothing of the distance, blind to even the majesty of the stars. He has never been a happy man, nor a fulfilled one, but something about this moment hurts in a brand new way. He realizes that only in utter defeat will he find his worth, only by burning what he's built to the ground will he earn true respect, and only by ending his own life can he prove the depth of his love.

Chest aching, he whispers, "I'm so tired," and Reyanne hears the echo of it in his thoughts.

THEN COME TO ME, AND I CAN GIVE YOU THE 'MORE' YOU SEEK! JOIN ME AND WE'LL END THIS WAR TOGETHER!

So naïve, princess.

And the endearment hits her harder than any insult ever could.

Zanth thinks, *Your people will kill me if I'm ever found. Why not die on my own terms?*

He prays the mirror gate will not open. If it does, he'll lose his resolve. Seeing her tear-streaked face through their connection last night nearly made him waver.

She begs him in sweet words, as if she could possibly care about him. Unfortunately, her emotions tell him she does... but it doesn't matter anymore. He's ready to do what he must.

Zanth takes his blade and positions it close to his throat. He can feel its dark, angry aura burn, uncomfortable heat searing his skin.

No, he scolds himself. *Not like that.*

His weapon would cauterize as it cuts, leaving him muted for life, but no more. That's not enough. Instead, Zanth wraps both large hands over his hilt as Reyanne wails within him, begging, pleading.

I pray you don't feel this, he tells her. *And I wish you success.*

With that, Zanth lifts his sword high in the air, angled just right...and drives the blade down and through himself in one heavy plunge. It strikes right where it was meant to, impaling the softness of his center, hopefully making his death a quick one.

The war will end now, Zanth sends, his vision blurring and pure shock muting any pain. *It will be alright, Reyanne. You'll see.*

She's weeping. Incoherent. She mourns him down to her bones...and maybe that's enough.

Zanth's dying words are, *This was for you.*

And he means it.

You, dear reader, have earned a SAD <u>ENDING</u>!

Remember, there are 17 possible endings, and this is just one. If you've found all eight Zanthrand endings, start back at the beginning, and choose Reyanne's path. Many diverging stories await you!

Good luck, dear reader!

CHAPTER 26

I can't move too quickly, he thinks to himself. *She's intelligent—no matter how desperate. If I turn from black to white, she'll know it's a trap. She's young and inexperienced, but she's not a fool.*

What Zanth has to do is set up intrigue and sympathy for himself. She needs to want to be close to him, to trust him, and it has to be her decision. They've had connections through their bond that weren't aggressive—either they were too tired or just not in the mood—and he just needs to recreate that paradigm. He needs to be patient. Soft. Vulnerable. The thought makes him sick but there are bigger things than him.

His people are tired. The warmongers of his council aside, his soldiers are scared to fight against any of the white witch's campaigns because she and Zanth are often the only ones left standing. His denizens are aching, weary of being separated from their families—both those who serve in the war and those who were carved out of the Dominion's citizenry due to nothing more than political circumstance, now stuck in the heart of the Separatists' territories whether they want to be or not.

Not only that, when the Separatists drew a line between what was Zanth's and what they insisted was theirs, many people were conscripted into the enemy's armies with no choice, something that leaves a sour taste in Zanth's mouth. He doesn't believe in conscription. Those who fight in Zanth's battles will be trained warriors and nothing less. The tradesmen, the farmers, and the feeble will not be thrown like meat to those dragon-riding rebels.

What's the first move? Zanth wonders, running a hand over his newly scarred face, feeling the hot throb of it. *Healing, I suppose. Replenishing my magic.*

And that's a good enough list to start with.

With that in mind, Zanth pulls his blankets up higher, letting himself doze and, finally, dream.

* * *

He slept for two days, and that was enough. Now, Zanth sits in his small library of occultist texts, several set out in front of him smelling like leather and old parchment—a dusty, comforting smell. His finger draws across one line before switching books and skimming another. They're telling him the same concept with different nuances. By combining aspects of six of these spells and two elixirs, Zanth's sure he can fix his eye. The medicines he'd been treated with have already sealed his wounds to purple scars, but his blindness is unacceptable. Battling with his peripheral vision cut in half isn't something he feels like dealing with if he can help it.

There is an echo of a murmur, and the energy in the

room shifts slightly, a charge of static in the air. Zanth sighs through his nose.

"I haven't time for you, white witch."

Turning over his shoulder, he sees the mirror gate has opened, letting him peer into Reyanne's chambers. She's yawning and sitting up from bed, scrubbing at her eyes. She takes one look at him and says, "Ugh!" before flopping back down onto her covers in distaste. "Why does it have to be you first thing in the morning?"

He turns back to his books, knowing she can do him no harm like this. There is a silence while he continues to formulate his healing spell, and he can feel her flutter over his brain. She never really *looks*, but she's like a child that jumps up and down in front of a tall wishing well. She can't quite manage to see all the coins, but you know she wants to.

Stop that, he puts into her mind. *Look or don't look, but don't aggravate me.*

He hears her groan, followed in short order by another yawn. Instead of digging deeper into his thoughts, she retreats completely. When he peeks over his shoulder again, she's reburied herself under the blankets.

He snorts in amusement. "I'm going to fix the eye you so happily ruined for me."

"Lucky I didn't kill you," she says, nasal and muffled from somewhere under a pile of goose down pillows.

"Am I, now?" He toys with the idea of several different ways to handle her presence, thinking of the long game of the ruse he's planning. In the end he settles on, "Would you like to help me?"

It's her turn to snort.

"I'd imagine it's the righteous thing to do," he adds.

"Don't push it," she grumps, her voice still swaddled.

"Otherwise, I'll be handicapped when we next battle."

"Wouldn't that be nice?"

"Come, come, Reyanne. Don't you want to beat me fairly?"

She pushes up on her hands, unearthing her head from the blankets and making her brown hair stand on-end with static. Green eyes narrowed, she frowns. "I'm always fair."

He lets a smirk grace the corner of his lips. "So you say."

He looks away, feigning disinterest, but feels her irritation percolate over their bond. She gets up on her hands and knees and crawls to the edge of the bed, clothes rumpled and skewed. Up now, she pads to the mirror gate and *thwams* a fist against it, though they both know that will get her nowhere. All she does is cause a small crackle of electricity to dance over the mirror's clear surface.

"What are you up to?" she accuses.

He gestures at his books. "As I said…"

She opens her mouth to say something of her own…and the gate closes.

Smiling, Zanth sends to her mind, *I'm guessing fate wanted you to keep those words to yourself.*

There's somewhere you can shove *those words,* she sends back.

So crass.

And she pulls away, likely to do her morning necessaries. It will give him some time alone then, which is good. He needs to concentrate to make this work.

Getting up, he proceeds to his personal apothecary. He happens to have one of the medicinal elixirs he needs already, and he's glad for it. It takes months to steep. Happily, the one he must still concoct isn't difficult. A half hour at most. Zanth's hands flit over his stores, bottles and carafes and boxes. Live and dead things. Things that skitter. Things that glow. Things that you eat and enjoy, things that you eat, and it kills you. So many unlabeled things. If someone were to wander into his haven, they'd either have to be very trained or not mind ending up very dead.

He selects a peacock feather and pulls off two strands, dropping them into his mortar. Next comes aloe. Next come coriame and thylight. A few organs of other creatures, including the last phoenix eye he has. If he mixes this elixir wrong, it will be difficult to obtain ingredients for another batch.

In it all goes, and he makes good work with his pestle, grinding it into a paste of gray guck, its scent a mixture of rot and sweet spices. He wrinkles his nose, wanting to gag, but there's nothing for it. The art of potion-making is not for the weak-stomached.

The finished elixir is in a dark, crimson decanter, more than enough for what he needs, so he takes a small measure together with his concoction and moves into his sanctuary. Zanth's chambers are widespread with many rooms, but they are sparse. He has not deigned to fill his life with finery, so his footsteps reverberate in the empty, high-ceilinged castle hallways. There are no paintings or tapestries. No unnecessary furniture or sculpted works. No pretense that he is anything other than what he is. Stark and alone with nothing to liven his barren existence.

The best place for magic is a small outer pavilion open to the sky with towering walls to keep the distractions from the city below to a ignorable murmur. Setting down his materials, he retrieves a bag of salt and begins to pour, drawing shapes and letters around the floor with the familiarity of a calligrapher. He has until the wind blows a grain out of place, which may not be very long at all.

Stepping carefully, he places himself in the middle triangle of three, his medicines in those to either side. With a whisper, flames burst into being beside him, warming the air, and Zanth begins to work his magic.

It's not a matter of memorization. It's understanding how the words call to the ether; how the music of it begs the universe to give you what you need. Of course, Zanth knows the simple spells one can parrot to get results, but he can also create magics all his own. In his lifetime, only he and Reyanne have possessed this talent. Not even his treacherous family could make such a claim. But because of his excellence, the words flow from him in elegant perfection. Hums and hisses. Hard "t"s and long "o"s. Sharp "ch" sounds and staccato syllables.

The universe calls for it, he knows, so Zanth's hands start to move. Fluidly, they slide over each other, drawing runes on his own skin that burn a blinding white, as if branding himself with the caress of sunlight. His ruined eye stings enough to make the whole one water in sympathy, but it doesn't matter. What's the worst that can happen at this point? If it's unsalvageable, then so be it.

Keeping the palms of his hands facing flat toward the stone, he chants, and his potions begin to glow lovely colors —amethyst and azure, like jewels in a crown. Taking a fingerful of each, he opens his blind eye and smears them in.

The pain is immediate, and Zanth's spell now comes through grit teeth. Something is happening. Something is changing.

It's working.

Suddenly, Zanth's neck loosens, his head lolling back as he gasps, his brain throbbing as he dips…

…into…

…a vision.

* * *

Zanthrand, bare-chested, is holding Reyanne of the White from behind, caressing the curve of her neck with his lips like a lover. One of his hands is snaked around her stomach and tucked between her legs and the other cups her breast. He sees it from outside himself, like an artist's rendering but all too real—pores and imperfections, clothing and textures, not to mention the motion of her quick breath as he tries to seduce her.

If she says yes, he'll take her as his queen.

If she says no, he'll fight her.

If they battle, she will die.

This is an undeniable truth—one he can't unsee.

The vision…

  … flips…

    …from future to past.

Seth Cassian, his exiled uncle and master of the dark arts, holds Zanth's throat in his hands, squeezing his larynx. It's not the first time someone close to Zanth has tried to kill him, but all the years of overdue vengeance are going to be exacted from this last, malicious monster.

The one thing Zanth's master had never learned was how to perform silent magic, but that is one of Zanth's secret specialties. As he struggles, his vision whitening with little pinprick stars, he points out his index and middle fingers, then retracts them. After a rotation of his wrist, his palm goes flat and draws a circle over his abdomen before he lashes out and *shoves* that hand against his mentor's chest.

Seth's screams are immediate, and Zanth revels in every pained note. When the man's grip loosens, Zanth drops like rocks crumbling on themselves, sprawling on the floor in a puddle of black robes and humiliation. Coughing and sputtering, he works to his knees, watching as his master bats at the inextinguishable fire now embedded inside him, boiling him from heart to skin.

"I hate you," Zanth says through bared teeth.

But Seth can't hear over his own crackles, his throat now glowing as flames flicker from his mouth like a dying dragon spitting the last of its venom. It's then that the rest of Seth ignites, and all struggle stops. The man *thumps* to his knees before landing straight on his face, sliding forward across the fine marble, and charring to ashen dust.

It's that simple. It's that fast. With one final spell, the head of the Dominion is dead.

Hand on his bruised throat, Zanth pants, gasping in the air he so deeply missed. His knights had seen everything, though the bastards never made a move to try to save him. Survival of the fittest, he supposes, and that title will always belong to Zanthrand.

He lurches to his feet, rolling his shoulders back despite the wave of dizziness, and stares his men down. Nearly as one, they drop to their knees, shouting, "Long live the Dark Moon!" which is what Zanth is now. What was once his master's now belongs to Zanth by divine edict. The whole of the Dominion is his to control. Like this, the vile Separatists don't stand a chance.

And for the first time in a long time, Zanth is satisfied.

Until…

…he goes back…

…even further.

Back to when his name was Brahm Jehanne.

A man just into his twenties, he had earned the rank of Sorcerer's Knight. His power with magic, both dark and light, had set him apart from the others in his cohort; he outclassed them all. It was this more than anything else that made his family mistrust him. Hate him.

Fatherless, perhaps by design, the triplet trifecta of his family—his queen mother and two talented sorcerer uncles —controlled every aspect of his life with cruel efficiency, demanding perfection or doling out punishment. Brahm had never been loved, but he had been taught, and he exceeded every expectation to the point of becoming a threat to his mother's power. Queen Annora Jehanne looked holy and pure from afar but, once you got close, you could see her for what she really was. Ruthless.

Of course, Brahm didn't know that at the time. It was only later that he would come to understand his family's true treachery—long after his uncle Seth was banished for being too kind to him. Too indulgent. Too permissive of Brahm's dark tendencies, which Seth himself had shared in secret.

Before Brahm's ascension to Knight, his other uncle, Leif, was the most powerful sorcerer in the lands. Leif had defeated monsters and mayhem, toppling the old Empire with stealth and cunning. Yet now, he's been eclipsed, bested by his nephew protégée at every turn. Other candidates for knighthood proved their worth merely by holding their own against Brahm's uncle, yet Brahm won his title by almost destroying him.

The young man was intelligent enough to keep his darkness in its place, however, overpowering but not obliterating. His uncle had been trapped on all sides by a shrinking barrier, unable to escape Brahm's magic. Leif struggled for hour after humiliating hour as the walls closed in on him, and when it became clear he would find no counter spell, the venerated war hero tapped out, fury readable on every inch of his face. To Brahm's credit, his uncle was released without a scratch on him, except for a deep gash ripped through his ego, perhaps. And perhaps that's why he felt Brahm had to die.

So now, Brahm is coughing out blood. His hands shake as he looks into his uncle's pale blue eyes, nothing but disdain laced with hate staring back.

"You made me do this, Brahm," he says. "The evil in you is

too strong."

"I…" Brahm tries, but it devolves into coughs, his lungs filling with wet warmth.

Leif looks at the bottle of poison in his hand. "You almost escaped me. Do you know how many times I've tried to do this?"

He doesn't…and Leif Cassian doesn't say anything more. He lets the vial tumble through his fingers and leaves Brahm exactly where he lured him, in a ditch outside the castle walls.

Brahm is fading. Fading….

But a small set of hands grabs onto his.

"Hold on!"

Blinking, he sees the blurred sight of a child picking up the bottle and smelling it, wincing at its odor.

"You didn't drink this, did you?" Hands pat Brahm's face. "Ohh. You did."

There is a sigh.

"Hold on," the child says. Muttering to itself, it scrounges on the ground. A trap door of sorts lifts, and the figure drops under it with an *oomph.* Brahm's consciousness is ebbing, but he fights, rolling over to allow the blood to drool from his mouth rather than choking on it. He grabs onto the mud and clenches, trying not to lose the will to breathe.

The figure pops out again, running its forearm over its face with a "Phew!"

Brahm feels something press onto his back outside his fine garb. The new robes his mother had given him. The ones his uncle said he looked so handsome in…

The press against him is firm, and it becomes hot in short order. Not unpleasant, calming more than anything, it radiates through his spine, his heart, ebbing into his chest.

"Don't move. This will take a minute."

The child ducks down into its secret place again, and

climbs up with something else, putting it in Brahm's mouth and making him bite down. All he tastes is iron, but what he feels in his mouth is spongy, as if he'd eaten moss.

"Swallow. It'll get stuck, I know, but make it work."

Beyond the ability to reason for himself, Brahm does as he's told by this—what, ten-year-old? He doesn't even bother chewing. He sputters and swears as some goes up his nose, but he keeps working his throat until he gets it down.

Immediately a wave of nausea hits him.

"Gonna—" he gets out before vomiting. The child holds that warm thing against his back even harder as his stomach knots and coils, thrusting everything he's got through his gullet. He's laying in the muck of it, but there's nothing to do but let his belly own his every bodily function as he contorts and curls in on himself.

"That's it. Get it alllllll out," the child says. It shifts Brahm's hair off his forehead with a tenderness that no one has shown him in years. Perhaps a decade. Perhaps longer.

Finally, his stomach has no more, and the dry heaving subsides. "W-who?" he tries.

"No one. Just a girl."

He somehow smirks. He's always had a way with girls, no matter the age. They like the dark, brooding type, as if it's been bred into them.

"Why?" he says this time.

"Why wouldn't I?" She sounds offended. "Is this still hot?" She presses firmly down on the hard thing against his back to the point of making him wince. He realizes that, no, it's not. He shakes his head weakly, his eyes clearing enough to see her properly. She is pure dirt, head to toe, and smells like earth. Her hair is brown, but whether that's filth or natural coloring, he has no idea.

Removing the item, Brahm sees that it's a rune stone. Those are rare. She holds it up to the sunlight and squints one eye shut, her tongue sticking out. "Yeah, that one's done." She tosses it behind her and mopes. "It was a good one, too."

Brahm doesn't dare move, though he's starting to feel better. "How did you get that?"

She shrugs. "I find them. They call to me."

"You must be a mage."

"Pffffft," she says, rolling her eyes. "That's not real."

He'd *pffft* back at her if he had the strength. All he can do is gesture slightly, sending a spell in the direction of what she'd thrown away. Immediately her eyes go wide, and she whips behind her, retrieving her stone.

"Is it fixed?!"

He mumbles his agreement. "I fixed it."

He tries to sit up, but she smooshes him down again, yelling, "Perfect!" and smashing the thing on his back once more, making that warmth return. Slowly, Brahm feels like he's knitting back together from the inside.

The child chatters. "I find these all the time. Sometimes they have marks on them, like this one, but I can't read, so I dunno if they say anything good. Sometimes they're plain, too. Either way, I've gotta test 'em to see what they can do before I wreck something by mistake. Sometimes their song tells me, though. That's how I know them for what they are. It's like what I think stars must sound like. Can you hear their songs?"

Brahm shakes his head, still laying in his own vomit, something he wants to change as soon as possible. Waving her off, he sits up, grimacing as he tries to push his filthy hair out of his eyes.

"Hey! Stay still!"

She *thwams* the thing over his chest this time, holding it against his breastbone and letting it warm him from the front. Huffing through her nose, she looks at him as if he's an idiot...and he probably is. He didn't see any of this coming.

"You shouldn't eat or drink stuff when you don't know what it is," she scolds him. "Otherwise, you could die. Didn't anyone ever teach you that?"

Brahm sighs, resting his head back on the castle wall. The shadows lean on them here on the far side of the city, a place where no one comes unless they want to be near the cliffs. His uncle had lured him to see the sunrise backlight the castle in a special way and offered wine to celebrate his knighthood. He'd made it seem like it was a special moment, one where he'd truly begin to see his nephew as a man instead of a boy, a hero in his own right, an equal. But that never happened…

And Brahm wants to kill something.

The stone on his chest stings then, and the little girl drops it with a cry. It lands harmlessly between Brahm's legs.

"Ouch! Whad'it do *that* for?!"

Eyeing it, Brahm realizes he must have had a well of darkness rise in him. Not good for white magic artifacts.

"Awww… It's dead again." The girl picks it up and looks at it, twisting it this way and that, pouting. With a frown, she thrusts it at him, demanding, "Fix it."

Brahm chuckles. He can't help it. Calming himself with a deep breath, he touches his fingers to the stone, encouraging it to sap more magic from the air all around them. "If you'd wait, they'd regenerate on their own. They just need time."

"Whaaaat?!" Her eyes go wide. "Do you know how many of these things I've thrown away?"

He outright laughs. "You should take better care of your witch's tools, my young apprentice. Magical artifacts are hard to come by."

Her lips part as her little mind gets blown. "Witch?!"

He ignores her. "And these all do different things," Taking her stone in his hand, he flips it over. "When mages find out their power, they're marked. See, this carved symbol means *salvation.* There are also ones for destruction, cold, heat—all sorts of things."

The little girl narrows her olive green eyes. "How do you know all this?"

He *thunks* his head back against the castle wall again. "I'm a Sorcerer Knight."

For all that's worth.

His eyebrows lift. "Wanna see a trick?"

She nods so fast, clumps of dirt slough from her hair. He wants to bathe her. Instead, he holds his hand out, whispers a single word, and snaps his fingers. With a *pop*, little lights now twinkle like daylight fireflies around the girl's head.

He'd hoped to make her giggle or ogle, but instead, she turns toward him with the harshest of glares.

"You said I must be a mage?"

His eyebrows knit. "Yes…?"

"And mages are real."

"Yes."

She shoves his shoulder. "Then teach me magic. And I'll teach you not to eat stupid things. Fair trade." She holds her hand out to shake, as if this was the world's most serious agreement.

Smiling, he decides, "Why not?" Taking her hand, he pumps it up and down. "What's your name?"

"I don't have one." She looks away and her face scrunches up. "But don't name me! Everyone tries to name me like I'm a pet! I'll come up with my own name when I'm good and ready!"

Brahm doesn't lose his soft expression. He'd rather stay in this moment than think even a minute into the past or future. "Then you should name yourself after something bright and wholesome, like the sun. Aurora, maybe, or—"

"Don't name me!" she grumps.

"Or Dawn…"

"I hate you already!"

"Or Ray, like rays of sunlight!"

"No!" she waves him off. "I like Ann! I've almost completely picked it! I just need to say it out loud a few more times!"

"Hmm," he teases, leaning forward and mussing her filthy hair, only to receive a sneer in return. "Why not put them together? Why not call yourself—"

* * *

"Reyanne," Zanth whispers, coming back to himself.

Could it truly be her?

Head still tipped back, his blind eye opens—not so blind anymore. It feels odd, but its sight is more than perfect. Closing his undamaged eye, he lets the new one reign and notices that colors are brighter. More vibrant. A bird flies overhead and he can see a red trail it leaves behind, like a heat signature where it warmed the air for the flicker of a heartbeat before moving on.

Standing quickly, Zanth collects his things and proceeds inside. He sees the dim interior without issue; no need for his new eye to adjust to the difference in lighting. Setting everything down, he rushes to his mirror, wanting to see what it looks like. Is it ruined and red? Is it gored and ghastly? Grabbing the reflective glass in its handheld frame, he holds it up, hands shaking, and sees vermillion surrounding his iris and a gold-yellow within.

It…glows.

He blinks a few times to make sure it's not a trick of the light, then he tries closing his new eye and focusing with the old one. Either way, it doesn't matter. The magic inside his healed eye casts an eerie yellow glow over the crest of his cheek and the under-arch of his brow. It looks ghostly. Demonic. Terrifying.

What happens if he locks eyes on someone or something for too long? Will they be damaged? Burned? Cursed?

Smirking, he looks to the ceiling, feeling mischievous.

He proceeds to the guards outside his chambers, barking, "Bring me a prisoner to be executed. It doesn't matter who."

There is a moment's hesitation before the guards click their heels together, and one runs off on his errand. Zanth is careful not to look at either. He's got some experimenting to do before he ruins someone by mistake.

* * *

Reyanne, Zanth pushes into her mind, lying lazily in his bed after supper. At this point, he's finished his experimentation and found his eye powerful in its insight, but harmless otherwise. He's glad of it. Though it would have been interesting to destroy people at a glance, surely it would have backfired at some point. Like the king where everything he touched turned to gold, Zanth would soon see the people he needed crumble to ash under his fiery gaze. No matter how many precautions, it would only be a matter of time. Better to be blind in such a case.

Reyanne, he tries again.

Since when do you call me anything other than 'White Witch'?

He smirks to himself. *We need to speak.*

We're speaking now.

It's not enough. I want to see if we can open the mirror gate on command.

You act like I want to see you, she says.

He pauses and sends a thread of vulnerability to her through their bond. *You don't want to?*

She waits several heartbeats before responding, enough that Zanth wonders if she'd heard him.

I only want to see you on the battlefield, she says. *It's my responsibility to end you.*

And yet, you showed me mercy.

Yes, well, you didn't seem too keen on dying.

Zanth cocks his head to the side. *No. You didn't seem too keen on killing me. Even though I'm your enemy. Arch nemesis, if you will.*

He can feel her amusement.

She shows a hint of interest. *Who's to say we could even do such a thing, or that it wouldn't harm us, somehow? For all I know, you've found a lovely way to make my brain explode.*

He *pffts*.

That's not the glorious death I would give you, white witch.

Why assume any death would be glorious?

It is simply his way of life. Die in battle with a weapon in your hand and earn the reverence due to a warrior. Either that or die old in your bed as a wizened sorcerer with as many tomes of your knowledge as possible captured and preserved for the centuries to come. Anything in between is shameful. Reyanne would be put off by his beliefs, he knows, so he doesn't bother voicing them. He's long past the point of trying to convert her to his ways.

Still, Zanth wants her to help open their connection, and if there's anything she's shown him, it's that he's her biggest weakness. All he needs say is the word:

"Please."

And she hears him. It makes her heart ache, for when has the mighty Dark Moon ever asked for anything so kindly?

She says, *What do you want me to do?*

Think of me. Focus on me. On your desire to see me.

My what? Reyanne's brain stutters and he loves every moment of it. If teasing out her sense of embarrassment will embed him even deeper in her thoughts, he'll take it.

Lacing an unknown feeling through his words, he says, *And I'll think of only you. Of your face and the way your mouth moves when you speak. I'll think of the way you fight me. I'll imagine the way your body moves, Reyanne. Can you picture mine?*

And ohhh, does he detect a flash of desire? His heart flutters at the thought.

But then he grimaces. He was supposed to be luring her in to destroy her. This is going wrong. But if it works, victory will be his. Zanth just has to remember to play the long game. She needs to cooperate with him. Trust him. Meet him face to face of her own volition.

Can you see me in your mind's eye, princess?

Wherever she is, Reyanne trips over something and falls down, cursing him.

Don't call me that!

Why? You don't like it? Or you like it too much?

Irritation now. She's flooded with it.

He grins. This is the most entertained Zanth's been in quite a while. He lets her feel that from him next, and her mortification reigns supreme. She'd bury herself if she only could.

His thoughts wandering, Zanth's lips press into a straight line. *Tell me something. Your strength with rune stones—where did you learn it from? Did you have a master?*

Why? she gripes. *Looking for someone else to kill, or do you just want to fill a gap in your skillset?*

He snorts. *Did you, or didn't you?*

Her marbles roll around her head. *I barely remember. I was young. I think I helped someone, and they trained me for a few days. The rest I picked up on my own.*

Zanth swallows, his young-self clamoring for attention, though that man has long been dead. "Tell me about him," Zanth says aloud, trying to compel her through their bond.

Reyanne, being Reyanne, digs in her heels, refusing to obey. *How do you know it's even a 'him'? And aren't I supposed to focus on* you, *nightmaster? Make up your mind.*

Was it a him?

Even to himself, he sounds jealous and accusatory, though being jealous of his younger self is the epitome of foolishness —that is, if Reyanne was, indeed, that child from long ago. Part of him hopes she wasn't. Part of him hopes she was... and he knows without doubt that part's right.

Shut up, Zanthrand, she says, and with that, she stops responding.

* * *

Over the next few days, he focuses on coaxing her into willingness. Once he's successful, they give it a first try, nearly popping their brains as they try to force the mirror gate to open, failing miserably. The benefit is that Reyanne really wants to do it now. Seeing it as a new and exciting challenge to overcome, she's fighting just as hard as he is... which also means she's thinking about him as much as he's thinking about her. It's a bittersweet feeling, knowing their motives mismatch. She's a fool not to scan his mind for a hint of his upcoming betrayal. An endearing, naïve fool.

There is another war campaign and it's inevitable that Zanth and the white witch will clash. Perhaps any newfound affection will stay her hand, as planned, and let him outmatch her.

But is that fair?

Does it even matter?

She's the enemy, he reminds himself.

If his ruse is to get her to drop her guard, he's on the cusp of having her bare her throat. Yet he had promised her a glorious death, and that won't happen if she looks him in the eye, loses herself in sorrow, and lowers her sword.

The thought wrenches his heart.

He thinks back to a little girl with dirty hair who'd saved his life. The one who'd grown up to be his equal. The day to his night. "Rays like the sun," he murmurs to himself.

What is he doing?

If memory serves, he stayed with her for over a week, hiding in her shoddy lair under the rickety trap door. She had an uncanny natural talent for rune stones, and so he taught her ways to bring out their magic. How to recognize their Druid symbols. How to draw them in the air, amplifying their spell power to cast it against others. That was a crucial lesson in self-defense, one he felt a small girl on her own needed to learn.

She stayed filthy the whole time. So did he, for that matter. At first, the young Brahm Jehanne had been afraid to be caught if he left her secret hidey-hole, but after a while he had just grown reluctant to leave *her*. They slept in the cramped space, her head on his chest as Brahm tried to formulate his next move, knowing he was not safe there. He needed to find the uncle whom his mother had exiled. Seth. Together, they could put a stop to the queen's scheming ways. Rebuild the old Empire. Make it new and learn from past mistakes. The glory of it enticed him, and his vindictive nature sealed the deal.

In the end, Brahm Jehanne had run away in the night, not even able to face the girl he was abandoning. He told himself it was to keep her safe, because if she knew he was leaving, she may decide to follow, and where he was going was no place for children. It was a place to shred his old self into pieces and glue them back together into new shapes. Brahm Jehanne needed to become Zanthrand of the Dark, the Dominion's black magic sorcerer, and the little girl he mentored was left to suffer alone in his absence.

How did Zanth not put Reyanne's name to that young face from so long ago? He looked in the white witch's memories many times and saw her left behind by figure after faceless figure. Who would've thought that he himself would've been one of them? What would life have been like if he had just run away with that little girl and they had grown up in magic and mischief together?

The thought makes him scowl. It would be too much like siblings for his comfort.

For more than a decade, Zanth has been entrenched in Seth's fanaticism, focused on that to the detriment of all else. Now, Zanth wonders how much of what he believes came to him on his own and how much was just ground into his brain until it stuck?

Does it matter?

Does he care?

Regardless of the reason or the rightness, he does. For the first time, he considers that he could have been someone else. That the person he wants to be may not be the person he actually is. That what he does for the sake of the war he both instigated and inherited may be the wrong choice.

It's a series of harsh revelations. But what would he change? Where could he begin?

He wouldn't kill her.

Then what *would* he do?

The other half of his vision comes to mind. The one where he almost bedded his white witch. His fingers tingle with the urge to touch her like he did in his vision...and yet he also watched himself destroy her without a second thought. One brought him pleasure, and the other brought him pain. In one future she accepted him, the other she rejected him. Which future is he heading toward? Both? Neither?

He should've tricked her immediately. This is getting messy.

* * *

"We did it…" Reyanne's voice is pure awe as she stares up at the arced curve of the mirror gate, twinkling stars framing the window between them. Her face travels the line of it like a child's, a smile pulling at the corners of her mouth and slowly spreading into the biggest grin Zanth's ever seen. "WE DID IT!" She makes a high-pitched squeak and claps her hands together, the sharp sound echoing through the gate.

She's adorable. She's precious. She's *beaming.* Zanth tries to mimic her enthusiasm but it's beyond his capability.

"I don't think I've ever seen you this pleased," he says.

She cocks an eyebrow at him. "I wonder why that would be." And then she really sees him. Upon locking gazes with Zanthrand, her jaw drops. Her hand drifts to the crest of her left cheek. "Your eye… It glows."

"I'm aware."

"Is that what hurt so bad the other day?"

"Likely."

She grimaces, rubbing the side of her face in sympathy. After a moment of consideration, she tips her head, lips pursed as she squints.

"It suits you," she decides.

"Because it's demonic?"

"I was going to go with 'threatening.'"

He chuckles.

Reyanne drops to the floor in her chambers and the mirror follows as she folds her legs in crisscross, still at eye level with him even as she sits and he stands, making her look like she's floating in the air. "So, tell me, Sir Demon, why have we been slamming ourselves against reality to make this work?"

His eyebrows lift. "You didn't think to ask me before now?"

She shrugs. "I figured you were trying to trick me or something, but I was curious to see where you were going with it."

Not as naïve as he'd thought. He runs a hand through his hair at his temple. "I'm surprised you didn't dive in to see for yourself."

Her nose crinkles. "You know I don't like that. It's intrusive."

"I do it to you."

She scowls. "My point stands."

Her chest rises with a large breath as she takes a meditative pose, trying to focus and not lose their hard work. He joins her on the floor and matches her posture, something she seems to take pride in.

"So why are we here, Zanthrand?"

Rubbing his fingers over each other, he feels their callouses. His mood sinks from triumphant to sullen. "Why didn't you kill me?"

She rolls her eyes. "What a stupid question."

"Then I'm a stupid man. Enlighten me."

She plucks at her trousers as if picking off lint. "I told you, you weren't ready to die."

"No. You weren't ready to kill me," he repeats. "But why? I'm your enemy. I destroy your armies. I am winning this war, for the numbers remain ever on my side and your mages are weakening. Once your barriers fall, the Separatist 'nation' is mine. I will eliminate your Queen and free my people from beneath her. So, I ask again, *why?*"

Her mood sinks to match his. He can feel his heart pick up because hers does.

"Would you like to hear an uncomfortable truth?" she asks. After a pause, "I don't know who I am without you."

Her gaze drops to the ground and will not lift. Zanth feels the burn of shame come from her side of the bond while he is stunned by her admission. These are words he would never allow himself to say aloud.

Until now.

Risking it all, he admits, "I feel the same."

And in saying those words, he knows killing her is off the table. Perhaps it always was; he just liked to pretend otherwise.

Her eyes glisten. "It's not the same. You have people who look to you for counsel. I have no one. I am a figurehead with no power. I am a fighter without friendship. I am a threat without trust. I want to blame you and how you're always listening through my ears, but it's not just since I've known you. My entire life has been like this. No one has ever wanted me unless I was of use to them. If I'm not fighting you, if either side wins the war, what then? What worth do I hold? The only one bound to me is you," —her voice drops— "and you want nothing do with me."

Zanth's heart pangs for his own reasons, guilt swelling in his chest. Words fill his mind. What to say. What not to say. Whether or not to roll over and expose his belly. For the first time in a long time, he feels out of his depth.

He straightens his back. "I refuse to be close to people. Everyone betrays me. My family tried to kill me, my knights are waiting in line, and there are a litany of mages on your side that used to be 'loyal' to me. Loyalty is a lie; there's no one I can trust. All I know is to be prepared. I must look around every corner and be ready to defend myself in every way possible, always on edge in case the next attack is coming from behind, but you..."—he leans in closer to the pane that separates them—"You're the only one who can't surprise me. I'm in your mind. I know your moves and motives before they even become clear to you, like I watch them form. Even as enemies, I trust you to be exactly what I sense you are. If you mean to hurt me, it's clear. If you mean to try to persuade me, it's obvious. I don't have to watch my back, Reyanne. I only need watch you."

Her cheeks tint pink. Clearing her throat, she dodges that part of the conversation. "I see why you think the way you do. And I'd already known your family tried to kill you." Reyanne taps her temple, indicating their connection and shared secrets. "Why, though? Who were they?"

The words are jarring. "You don't know?" he asks. She looks on the verge of being defensive, so he holds up a hand to stop her. "They never told you?"

"Told me what? Who's 'they?'"

"My uncle tried to kill me at my mother's command. I had just been dubbed a Sorcerer Knight only to be poisoned by the very man who taught me all I knew."

She narrows her eyes at him, shaking her head in confusion.

"Your venerated Leif Cassian, my white witch. Your Separatist high mage. *That* is the man who tried to end me before I'd committed a single sin."

Reyanne's eyes go as wide. *"He's* your uncle?"

Zanth nods.

"But that would make your mother..."

Leaning in further, he smirks meanly, his new eye darting over every inch of her. He can see the quickening pulse in her veins, the emotional sweat in all her crooks and creases, the temperature dropping in her face as she feels lightheaded.

"But Brahm Jehanne died!" she argues.

"You're not wrong." Thrusting himself up from seated position, he begins to pace, the urge to fight taking over anything else.

"Zan!" she yells, and he looks over to see the mirror gate fading. She's holding the surface, palms flat on nothing but static as she watches the gate's edges begin to fade.

Stepping up, Zanth places his hands where hers are, unable to feel them, though he feels them all the same. He focuses on her. "Look at me, Reyanne."

"Zan, don't let it close!"

"I don't want it to," he says, and he means it.

Fear owns them both, creating lumps of loneliness in their throats.

"Focus," he says. "Tell me the first memory you have of me."

There is a warbling sound in the air as reality tries to close in on itself. The mirror's electricity crackles between them, but they cannot truly feel it. All they can feel is the pull from one to the other. If their connection ran deep before, it feels all-encompassing now.

She swallows. "I was standing on a bridge with my soldiers behind me. It was my first battle and all I'd heard about was you. I feared none of the warriors in black that faced us down, but I knew enough to be afraid of you."

"What did I look like?" he says through grit teeth, the mirror sparking as it tries to let them go.

"You were taller than any man alive. You were stronger than any beast. You looked like a God of Death."

"That's right, princess. That's exactly what I am."

Urgently, she says, "Now it's your turn. Tell me of the first time you saw me."

He swallows heavily. "It was long before you bound us together. Before you saw me across the battlefield. You were a lonely girl who had no name."

Her mouth drops open.

Desperately, he tries to get out a rush of words. "You were a child living in the dirt who saved my life. A child who I—"

And the mirror gate shatters into nothing. Zanth stumbles in the void that remains, nothing left to hold his weight. He whips around in terror, wondering if their window will ever open again. Wondering if they broke it forever.

Longing now floods their connection; blind, endless longing that ricochets from one to the other, two hearts searching for a home and coming up empty. Wordlessly, she calls to him, and he feels as if he's going to weep because over on her side of the bond, she is.

The only reason I left you was because it wasn't safe! he calls silently. *They would have killed me, and you would have died if you followed! I didn't want to leave you behind!*

Come to me, she pleads. *Come to where our connection can't end.*

She's asking for him all on her own, just as he planned. It's exactly what he'd wanted, though he wants it for different reasons now.

Don't move, he tells her.

Zanth's voice is a low drone as he utters his most familiar spell. Everything about him seems to ebb, the edges of his fingers blurring as if he was powder being blown away. But he is not. He is smoke. Everything about him blackens, from pale skin to glowing eye, as he becomes a tumult of motion, dark mist roiling on itself. Like this, Zanth can go anywhere he likes. He is beholden to no law of man or God. He is smaller than ants, he is lighter than feathers, he is blacker than pitch, and in the moonless night sky, Zanth is less than a ghost as he speeds toward the Separatists' castle. The one

Brahm Jehanne grew up in. The one he almost died beside. The one where a lost little girl gave him back his future.

I'm coming.

* * *

There is no contest between Zanthrand and the magical barriers set by the Separatist mages. Not when he's like this. His particles slip through the surface like an airy breeze, no hint of his dark intentions detected. The turrets of his mother's stronghold aren't how he remembers them. They are moss-covered and unkempt, dirty and dragon-scorched now that the country is forced to put its housekeeping efforts toward more deadly, warmongering endeavors.

He can feel Reyanne though their bond like never before, tugging and pulling his soul to hers. They are in sync, their hearts fully connected, allowing him to easily drift through familiar open windows and down dark, regal hallways until he finds her like a beacon.

Her white staff is pointed at none other than his now-aged uncle. The man backpedals away from her holy blade, the weapon's light catching all his ridges and valleys in the worst of ways. The years have done Leif Cassian's face no favors, making him saggy and sallow.

How the mighty have fallen.

"Did you do it!?" Reyanne growls. "Did you try to kill Brahm Jehanne!?"

For that, Leif has no words. He just holds up his hand in supplication, taking a beat to collect his wits as she steps closer. Zanth hides in the eaves, watching, though she knows he's there. He feels her rage at his uncle rise in solidarity with his own.

"His power is not unlike yours, Reyanne," Leif tries. "Formidable. Ingenious. Instinctual. But it's tainted. He's evil. I knew it then and I know it now."

"If he is, it's because of you!"

A small woman cowers to Reyanne's left side, half hidden behind an elaborate curtain. Zanth knows that face. Round, with almond eyes so dark they're almost black. Coal-colored hair, long and straight, falling over her shoulders just so. Her thin lips are pulled into a grimace, hands clenched, unsure of what to do as she watches the life-or-death tableau before her.

Zanth swoops down and materializes directly behind her, looping his hand around to stifle her scream and whispering a hard, *Shh.* Pressing forward, Zanth half shoves, half drags the woman out into the open, and Reyanne casts a glance over her shoulder.

"Don't hurt Lilah," she says.

"I would never," he assures her. When he lets the woman go, she wheels around and goes pale. His name falls from Lilah's lips like a sigh of horror, as is the proper response. Zanth's cruel uncle stares with similar wide eyes, but the name he calls out is very different.

"B-Brahm?"

Reyanne's stomach drops when Zanth's does, the feeling compounding between them.

"Brahm Jehanne died a long time ago." Zanth steps forward to stand beside his white witch. "I am all that remains."

"Reyanne, what have you done?" Leif says, his accusatory eyes locked on hers, his uncle again assuming evil deeds of the innocent. The words seem to rend Reyanne's tender heart.

Unacceptable.

Zanth's voice drops as his fierce eye radiates golden light. "La'a yanth ekaat minoshi."

Leif yells, "Brahm, don't!"

"Apalam anot jekeel."

"Please!"

Zanth's new eye flashes. "Jer *sot!*"

And Leif is caught in that familiar magical barrier—the one he couldn't escape when Brahm locked him in it, once upon a time. The clear walls are shrinking as before, but much faster. This isn't just proof of Zanth's power anymore. This is raw intent to kill.

"Zan, what are you doing?" Reyanne asks, horrified. She knows the answer already. She can feel his bloodlust like a sickness.

"Don't look," is all he says, hovering his fingers beside her face as if he would caress her. "For your sake, my white witch, I will not let you hear a single scream. Yet I shall take pleasure in every last one."

And he tenses his fist, sending Reyanne spiraling into unconsciousness.

Catching her easily, he holds her like a damsel as he stares his uncle down. Leif's eyes are wild as he beats against his shrinking container, looking for a weakness. He's in perfectly embroidered bedclothes, ineffective runes of protection threaded into every inch. Zanth wonders if the man had sewn them himself with his failing magic or if the Separatists' mages are in fact much weaker than advertised.

Slamming against surfaces that only contract, the old man lets out animalistic grunts and growls as he tests his physical limits. Zanth's new eye can see the sickly squeeze of Leif Cassian's heart as it thumps its terror center stage in the depths of his heavy chest. It would give him a heart attack in the near future if only he were to live that long.

"Master Zanthrand," Lilah says, her voice tight and terrified. Her gaze flicks from Leif to Zanth and back.

"My wonderful spy. When this is done, you will get us out of this castle. And then, you may have your sister back."

"Anika?" Lilah says, a high pitched little yip of hope.

Zanth won't take his eyes off his uncle, who is now ducking his head. "I promised, didn't I?"

And Lilah, who has fed scroll after scroll of intelligence to the Dominion over the years, places a hand over her mouth as she lets out a happy sob. That is all she's ever wanted, and she will have more than earned it.

"Brahm!" Leif screams. "Brahm, you can't do this!"

"Oh, but that's where you're wrong. I could have done this long ago, yet didn't out of love. Now, though? Now I just want to watch you die. And unlike you, I will not walk away like a coward. I'll make sure you are irrevocably, utterly, eternally destroyed. There's no one coming to save you."

Like she did for me.

Cradling Reyanne, Zanth watches his uncle start to froth, screaming obscenities as he's forced to his knees, his palms braced against the top barrier as he tells Zanth exactly what he thinks of him. Every word is a song that Zanth has longed to hear, his uncle's fury and helplessness payback for all the years Zanth struggled alone.

Anger turns to panic as Leif is reduced to a crouch, balling himself smaller and smaller as the box shrinks in. And in. His mouth spits spells end-to-end, praying for some last-minute miracle, but none find their way. It's only when Leif Cassian feels the invisible press of magic against every side of him that he begins to beg.

For all his talk, Zanth's not sure he likes this part. Reyanne has awoken some kind of empathy in him, and he finds his uncle's blubbers now pull at the little conscience he has left. Emphasis on the word *little.*

Lilah refuses to watch as Zanth draws a line in the air, silencing any sounds coming out of the shrinking barrier. That's why he doesn't hear it when the first bone breaks. He doesn't hear *any* of them break. But he sees them.

Splintering, they become jagged edges that deform his uncle's skin into terrible, unnatural lumps. They breach the surface, blood coating the fine floor in the red of pain. And when Leif Cassian cannot possibly get any smaller, punctured at all angles by his own shattered insides, only then does Zanth allow his barrier to release, making what's left ooze sideways in a deflating puddle.

Lilah loses her stomach on the marble floor, but Zanth does her a kindness. Approaching, he sets his hand on her forehead and whispers, stealing the moment's memories away.

Ensuring she's not looking at the mess Zanth has made, he tells her, "Now get us out of here."

And Lilah complies.

* * *

One last spell out of his system, the smokey form of Zanth rests in a decanter at Reyanne's hip with Lilah leading her through the castle as if nothing had happened. In truth, in either woman's mind, it hasn't—and all for the better. Long-held desires that owned Zanth have been sated, ones he's waited a decade to satisfy. Thankfully Reyanne doesn't dig around in his mind, so she will never have to know.

Even after such a horror, Zanth feels relief, like a tight leash has fallen away. His darkest demons died tonight, and Zanth will never be haunted again.

He has until sunrise to stay in this form. His spell only

works at night, so he must be out of the castle and beyond the magic wards by then or he may have to slaughter his way out. His white witch may have allowed him a certain level of forgiveness for being the enemy, but that level of destruction is something her good conscience will not abide. He'd prefer not to fight her ever again if he doesn't have to. He has new plans now.

Zanth has a true ally in Lilah, however—no matter how unwilling. He's kept her sister, Anika, for years, not quite in a dungeon, but in a beautiful set of rooms she cannot leave. One where no one comes to call. One where food can easily be withheld. Yet Anika and Lilah exchange letters, and through these, Zanth has learned many wonderful things. In truth, Lilah is one of the key things winning him this war. It's a shame to lose her as a source of intelligence, but Zanth is a man who keeps his word…and the fighting will be over soon, anyway.

Tunnels bring them outside the magic barrier with Zanth still in his disembodied form. The minute they're beyond the final seal, Zanth escapes his confines and bursts back into shape, grabbing Reyanne's hand and pulling her into a blind run. If she minds, she doesn't say, silently or otherwise. For Zanth's part, he's oddly ecstatic to touch her.

For days, they travel, seeking shelter in all of Zanth's secret strongholds along the way. Reyanne's clothes have been altered into something appropriately dark—Dominion attire—and her growing unease sits heavy in Zanth's soul.

One more step, he tells her.

And what is that?

Zanth takes a deep breath as they near his castle gate, the morning sun shining. *I give the command to end this war.*

Reyanne's anger sinks into his very bones. *And then you'll bring about your reign of terror.*

No, Zanth tells her. *That's when I'll dissolve my council, give them their spoils of war, and reunite my lands. Then the healing can begin.*

The Separatists' people will never accept the Dominion, she says.

Perhaps. Yet knowing that the White Witch has pleaded with the Dark Moon to show mercy will matter. And when they learn that she will be married to solidify a treaty of peace, what can they do but comply? They will not fight against their beloved hero.

She looks at him as if he's lost his mind. *That...*

'That' what?

That's the worst marriage proposal I've ever heard!

He chuckles, drawing Lilah's attention. "Lilah, what's the most surefire way to end a war?"

The woman rolls the question around in her mind, her thin eyes narrowing. "Conquest, trade treaties, or marriage."

"Smart girl," Zanth praises. Looking pointedly at Reyanne, he smirks. "I can accomplish all three."

Reyanne scoffs. "Queen Jehanne will never allow it."

"Thankfully, my dear, with the spell I was able to set inside the castle walls, her life is already forfeit."

Both women look at him, jaws dropping. Zanth merely raises his eyebrows.

"What's worse," he asks, "killing hundreds or killing just one? People will take it as a sign from the Gods."

Even Reyanne has to concede the point. Nodding firmly, she sets the grim reality in her heart: this is the way to end the war. Oddly enough, she doesn't seem to mind the Queen's demise like Zanth thought she would. Instead, she feels a dark sort of relief. She laces her fingers through Zanth's, squeezing tightly.

And I won't be left behind? she asks meekly.

He gazes at her out of the corner of his eye. *Never again.*

A slight blush rises to her cheeks even as she frowns. "Fine. If it's for the greater good, I'll marry you. But only if we can be equals. I refuse to be locked away in some bridal tower for your eyes alone."

He snorts at the very idea. "Agreed, princess. Alongside me, the Dominion is yours. We'll create a new era of peace."

Taking one more step forward, the guards see Zanth's face and regalia, immediately standing at attention and opening the barrier between his trade road and the rest of his capital city. Soon to be *their* city. The Dominion is about to have its first Queen. Zanth knows, then and there, that his dreams have finally come true, ones he'd held in his most secret heart.

He runs his fingers through Reyanne's hair, feeling warmth bloom in her chest. "You're perfect. Did you know that?"

She smiles shyly. "And you...are tolerable."

He smiles along with her. Dragging her close, he stops walking, and lets his lips hover over hers. "Keep that sassy mouth, my white witch. I find I like it when you challenge me."

He kisses her then, and her body goes loose in his arms, making him hold tighter. She's so innocent. So sweet.

Absolutely perfect, he tells her again. And, wonder of wonders, she feels...happy. It makes him happy, too.

You, dear reader, have earned a <u>HAPPY ENDING</u>!
One of two in the Zanth track! Good job, you!

Remember, there are 17 possible endings, and this is just one. If you've found all eight Zanthrand endings, start back at the beginning, and choose Reyanne's path. Many diverging stories await you!

Good luck, dear reader!

CHAPTER 27

rick her now, he thinks. Otherwise, his maliciousness will bleed into the story he's weaving, he's sure of it.

Sitting up, a deep pang runs through his head. He focuses, though, and with a slow wave through the air, a scroll appears, ashen and seeming to glow an eerie red. It's perfect. There's no mistaking that this comes from him. His five fingertips touch the paper and swipe quickly down the rough surface, capturing the whole of his thoughts in one stroke.

Reyanne of the White,
Our recent encounter leaves me unsure. Uncomfortable. Unsatisfied.

A truth.

I require a conversation that the bond cannot

break into pieces. Somewhere I can look at your face and show you my expressions, the one thing our mental connection never offers.

You can bring weapons if you will not trust me, but it is not my intention to battle against you.

Half-truth. There will be no battle. Only her demise.

The time is the next full moon.

Mere days away. She'll never suspect his magic will have restored so quickly, but dark magic works much differently than white. He doesn't always need to wait to be replenished; sometimes he takes what he deserves.

Choose a place. As long as it's not behind your castle walls, I will trust you. No warriors. No mages. Just us.
Decide.
Zanthrand
Dark Moon of the Dominion

He seals it with his blood, a thumbprint pressing the coagulating red into shape. Running his lips over it, he whispers, ensuring none but her will be able to see it, never mind read it. Touching it to his forehead, he embeds within its surface a sense of his urgency, an attempt to confuse her with the strength of his will.

He summons his owl then. Ergol. A beautiful bird with beautiful brown markings. It hoots softly as Zanth slips his magical message into the pouch fastened around the bird's neck. "Take this to Reyanne of the White. Be neither seen, heard, nor felt. Swift and silent, little one."

The owl lets out a chitter of understanding, fluffing the feathers around its neck until they puff up adorably. Zanth runs a hand over his pet, crown to tail, and wishes it good luck.

* * *

In the middle of the night while the white witch sleeps, Zanth meets with his war council. Alec Schezain, one of the Dominion's many generals, stands with a hand respectfully over his heart.

"Master, single combat is never a good idea."

"Did I ask your opinion?" Zanth intones, danger in his voice.

Schezain audibly swallows. "No, Master. But protocol states we send a contingent—"

"Which I do not require. Or do you doubt my skill?"

Doubt it or not, no one would dare speak such a thing aloud.

Zanthrand's strategists sit at a long table, Zanth himself at the head. Today he is in deep, royal blues, a color Reyanne has never seen him in. The finery of his clothing has been enhanced beyond simple brocade. Strands of pure gold weave the pattern now, making him look more a king than an agent of dark magic. It seems the shift in costume equates to a shift in tone, encouraging his people to speak up against his plan. He'll let it go…for now. If those close to him, the ones who consider him most deadly, are affected by something as trivial as hue, Reyanne is sure to feel the same.

Zanth stands, resting his fists on the tabletop and leaning his weight on them. "You don't need to know my plan," *for I dare not speak it aloud.* "You do not need to know my location," *because the white witch has yet to give it to me.* "But in three days, the full moon will rise, and I expect you to press further into the Separatists' territories in my absence. Cut through their flank. Now more than ever is the time to strike."

At this, Schezain smiles. "My weapon, master?"

Zanth nods. "If we're to use it, this would be the perfect time."

While I have her distracted.

* * *

Two days, and Reyanne has yet to respond to his message. Worse, she has blocked him from her mind.

He knows exactly what she's doing. She's brewed a sleeping draught to keep her in stasis until the time of their meeting, hiding her thoughts from him the only way she knows how.

"Foolish," Zanth says aloud to his owl, scritch-scratching beneath its beak. "If she'd pried into my thoughts, she may have figured out my plot in time."

The bird nibbles his finger too hard and Zanth lets it draw blood. Ergol is a predator, after all, just like Zanth himself.

"Shall we look into the white witch's dreams, little one?"

He finds he misses her verbal intrusions on his mind and

longs to provoke her, if for no other reason than to get her attention. He seems to be unexpectedly needy in his solitude, no matter how short a time it's been since he last heard her.

Ergol's tongue flicks against the wound it's given him—whether to soothe it or to taste the flesh it cannot have, Zanth's not sure.

With a smirk, he works his way over to his overlarge bed. Plush with the softest of furs, it keeps the warmth alive in an otherwise cold room. His bird has done him a favor, pricking his finger, and Zanth draws the blood over his forehead in a familiar rune pattern.

Closing his eyes, Zanth feels himself drift above. A haze of mental magic renders him unable to see from his one good eye, the other already blanked out to blackness—something he absolutely has to heal, but not until after he's garnered every inch of the white witch's sympathies.

Reyanne, he calls to her in the heavens. Amorphous shapes begin to take hold of his internal vision, bringing him into the nonsensical, clouded world of her dreams.

Leif Cassian—Zanth's betraying uncle—the man who once tried to poison him—stands, mouthing inaudible shapes until his words catch up in an echo. His facial flutters and tenor refrain overlap incorrectly, as if time has been torn apart and stitched together wrong, reassuring Reyanne that "you don't have to do this…"

When Zanth turns his head to find her, he sees that Reyanne is but a child in this section of her mind, hunched in on herself, dirty and rocking in a desolate, unlit corner. Her words, unlike Zanth's uncle's, are as clear as glass: "I have to trust him. This might be the key to ending the—"

And the vision…

        …mists, leaving Zanth in a new setting. It's the white witch's colorful bedroom of quilts and pillows. Firelight and warmth. An inversion of the icy, regal tomb he's sealed himself in.

"Zan," she whispers—but it's not fearful or angry. It's seductive. Dream-Reyanne opens her eyes and gazes at him, heavy-lidded and red-lipped, her mouth parted as if she might say more.

He suddenly wants her to say more.

Somehow suspended in the air of her dreamscape, Zanthrand cascades toward her in a billow of crimson smoke, not needing to move a muscle to do it. Floating, his garb wafts behind him in watery flutters as he reaches down to wrap his hand around the nape of her neck. Sliding his fingers through perfectly disheveled hair, he lifts her slightly and hovers close enough to kiss her. To bite her.

"Why are you dreaming of me, princess?" The endearment comes out unbidden.

She gasps as if he'd touched her secret spots, eyes slamming shut as she arches her body. Something inside him aches and longs to connect. Mouths, hearts, and lower.

The whole of her atmosphere swirls red with danger and lust as she licks her lips like a succubus about to suck him dry. At this moment, he'd be willing. Part of his subconscious dances with hers now.

"Take me," she whispers.

But...

...the scene...

...shifts...

...and suddenly Reyanne is standing in front of her Queen, Annora Jehanne. Zanth couldn't hate that woman more if he tried. Not just his enemy, but his once-mother stares at Zanth's white witch with unending disdain.

"Failure," his mother accuses, her lips tight. Zanth had heard that word many times in his young life.

His mother growls, "You'll never be good enough. A constant disappointment. Shameless and shameful. Stupid and stunted. You only learn when I hit you."

Zanth and Reyanne flinch in tandem. Is his mother still talking to her? Or is she talking to him? His heart is twisted up in the white witch's dream. Or is it his dream? Is he tainting this faux reality with his memories, or is this a true fear Reyanne holds in her heart?

"Please," she begs. "Please don't hate me. Please don't leave me behind. I'm sorry!"

Tears roll down her cheeks. The sudden wetness makes her face crumple inward, like tissue paper dissolving. Her nose disappears and her eyes are being gobbled up as her ears pull toward center. Her arms begin to twist at odd angles, square snaps and circular squiggles. It's hilarious. It's ludicrous. It's terrifying.

What in the hells is happening?

* * *

Zanth sits up sharply in his bed, breathing in a panicked, staccato rhythm. Night has long past fallen and he is covered in sweat. Scrubbing his hands over his cheeks and up to his forehead, he rubs off whatever dried blood crackles remain. Joining her in dreams is dangerous, no matter when or where, but today was…

His knuckles go white as he clenches his hair, willing his heart to slow down. This has not gone well. If any empathy exists inside him, he feels it now. If desire is a sin, it's raging between his legs. If shame about his trickery is possible, it sings a deadly song in his mind.

He doesn't have time for this. The plan is to kill her.

That's always been the plan. If it takes him down with her, so be it. General Schezain's weapon will win them the war. It's more blood than Zanth had wanted to shed, but he's tired of this dance. So are his people.

Still, Reyanne's image lives behind his eyes. The child. The temptress. The failure. The woman who unmade herself with sorrow. He hurts on her behalf. Not because the bond is forcing him to, but because he simply can't help himself.

"What have you done to me?" he whispers, even though she cannot hear.

* * *

One day left, yet Reyanne still hasn't responded to his message. He's going crazy. He dared not enter her dreams again, but he'd gleaned enough to know that she's planning on meeting him, despite the opposition from her leadership. With the crown standing against her, however, perhaps *she's* not the one keeping herself asleep and disconnected. Perhaps *they* are.

The thought enrages him.

Come to me, white witch. Come to me now.

He pushes the thought through their bond, even if it falls on deaf ears. There's a chance she'll sense him, and that may be all she needs to wake up. He needs her, one way or the other.

* * *

Reyanne's voice in his mind is small and weak, reaching

him when the sun rises. He had barely slept. Tonight is the full moon, yet until this morning, he'd had no word from his obsession. Finally sensing her thoughts trickle into him makes his hot blood cool into something resembling calm.

I will meet you, she says. Succinct.

Where? he sends back, threading it with urgency and, dare he say, hope. But for what, he's not so sure anymore.

The valley of Ethereum.

A white magic stronghold if ever there was one. Still, the night would be his. A compromise.

At moonrise, he reminds her.

He can feel her trepidation even as she agrees, and then she falls unconscious once more.

* * *

Having her mind touch his again did something to him, he swears. As the day goes on, he gets increasingly agitated the longer she stays silent. Will she be in any condition to fight? Will her death be an empty one? Does he care? Does he even want to kill her anymore?

Zanth grunts as he shoves himself into his new, blue fighting garb, still planning to throw her off with attire that looks less like night itself.

If I don't kill her, then what?

Unbidden, images of her beneath him and gasping at the sound of his voice come to mind. Every movement in his body stops, his arms in crisscross as he works to loop a tunic over his neck. The corners of his mouth drag down as he swallows, yanking the damn thing around his torso and trying to banish the thought, trying to focus on the other, sadder, more terrifying aspects of the dream…but he can't.

If she's asleep, can he sate his lust on his own? It may be the only way to slake his thirst so that, when he sees her, he doesn't swallow her whole.

* * *

The vestiges of the setting sun cast a slight orange over the otherwise pale valley of Ethereum. Its short, almost mossy grass has been bleached by the white magic infiltrating its every molecule. Every shrub looks as if it's covered in snow, even in the heat of summer. The animals that dine here have long lost their pigment, their eyes turning an albino red over time. After generation upon generation, Ethereum's native species are now simply born devoid of color, from tiny ants to rugged elk.

Zanth's black Pegasus looks like a dark bullseye in a place like this. Still, Zanth would ride no other. Stilte and he share their own kind of bond just like he and Ergol do, one of understanding and respect for one another's nature. His pegasus is pure calm so long as Zanth is safe. Danger, however, makes the mare bite and rear, flapping her wings and beating anything and everything away. She has become fearless in battle, allowing Zanth to swoop down on his enemies from above, swinging his heavy blade to remove heads and hands with one stroke. When soldiers clash, Stilte is out for blood just as much as Zanth, her wings and hooves truly a thing of beauty as they knock enemies to the ground, sometimes with caved-in faces.

His airborne steed lands him far enough from Reyanne as to not be threatening. The white witch has borrowed a dragon from the Separatists' stables, no doubt, but the beast is currently nowhere to be found. Clucking his tongue,

Zanth pats Stilte's haunches and lets her take flight, allowing his own method of escape to go to a distance. His heart yells *Trust*, which he does. He trusts he's at no risk here and fears no harm. Reyanne couldn't lay a hand on him if she tried, unarmed and unarmored, just as he'd asked. How very stupid.

"Zanthrand," she calls across the distance as he walks toward her. "How has something as simple as mercy confused you so?"

He hums in amusement, hands in plain view by his sides. "Why so quiet, white witch?"

Her head cocks to the side.

"Not here." Zanth taps his lips. "Up here." He taps his temple this time. "Have you planned some terrible demise for me?"

Her face falls from confusion into a kind of disturbance. He feels her debating what to tell him next, but already knows it was exactly as he feared.

"My people didn't want me to come," she says.

"Tried to tuck you away like Sleeping Beauty, did they?" Though the thought still makes him grind his teeth. The feeling seems mutual as her anger sizzles over the bond, her jaw tensing.

Cooling her emotions quickly, she says, "They only tried to save me from an untimely death. No one trusts you."

"They didn't trust you to best me, you mean."

Pulling at her plain garb, she says, "All that matters is that I trust myself."

He smirks at that. "How did you escape?"

She thinks for a minute, looking at him with something unnamable in her eyes. "I thought I heard your voice calling me. I felt conflict in you after I left you on the battlefield. I felt it through your letter, too. …And even right now."

Lips a pressed line, Zanth approaches still. "You're not

wrong."

Her shoulders droop—not in relief, but a kind of shyness, perhaps, her gaze going to the ground. "When I created the bond, I'd really only wanted to create this feeling in you. I wanted you to consider that there's more to life than anger and darkness."

"Yet there is violence in the light."

At that, her eyes glisten. "Even those in the right can be wrong."

"Your leadership?"

Reyanne worries her hands together. He remembers the other version of her from their shared dream. The one that crumbled in on itself at his mother's harsh words.

"You're stronger than this," he tells her, though he's not sure why. "Stronger and more powerful than any of them. No matter what they say or do, you can overcome them."

She huffs a sardonic laugh. "Always thinking of destroying, aren't you?

"It's in my nature." He's close enough now to touch her. She looks up, flicking her gaze from his lips to his eyes. Perhaps their dream is affecting her the way it's infected him. The look on her face is enthralling. Beautiful.

"Is there anything else in your nature?" she asks.

"So many things."

"Like what?" It comes out like a soft breeze. Something in him sparks at the sigh of it, and she can feel that emotion within him. Her eyes lock on his mouth again as he takes one last step toward her.

DEAR READER,

Does Zanth kiss her? Turn to page 188 (chapter 29)

Does he start a fight? Turn to page 182 (chapter 28)

CHAPTER 28

He raises his hand and latches onto her throat. "Like resisting temptation." Zanth whips his free palm to the side, fingers splayed as his blade materializes from nothing, its black metal glowing with an ominous scarlet haze as its familiar weight settles in his hand.

Her eyes narrow, her voice strained from the pressure on her larynx. "I thought this was going to be a peaceful chat."

"Your folly, truly." He shoves her backwards and she stumbles, catching herself at the last minute. "I told you weapons would be acceptable. You should have taken precautions. At least I've kept my word and brought no others. As I said, I have no plans to battle. Only to ruin. I am surviving this night, white witch, but I will be the only one."

He hates the feeling of betrayal in her heart, knowing that feeling all too well. His victory is already distasteful. Unbalanced. If he doesn't even the playing field by discarding his weapon, it will be an empty win, yet if he doesn't completely dominate, there is a chance he might lose.

He *cannot* lose.

"An enemy is an enemy," he recites once more—to himself as much as to her. "And enemies must be destroyed."

His shoulder tenses as he lifts his sword in a slashing arc, lunging forward to take a swipe at her. Her agility gets the better of him as she ducks and weaves, though she's too groggy and off her guard to think of a single spell. Her people shouldn't have kept her asleep for so long. She's no match for him like this.

Mercy. She'd shown him mercy.

But mercy is for the weak.

"The Separatists are a blight," he says, skipping over a kick she'd round-housed at him. His weapon stabs downward, catching a fluttering bit of her pale garb and tearing it into ragged rips as she dances away.

She calls back, "Queen Jehanne is the only thing saving those people from your tyranny!"

Dodging around to his blind side, she throws another kick his way, one he takes to the ribs before catching her foot and pulling her off balance, slamming her onto her back.

He can feel it in her mind. She's dipping into her stores of magic now, ready to fight back. Before she can complete a spell, Zanth pivots, falling upon her like a predator, a heavy hand clamping over her mouth and stopping her words.

"Your *Queen* is a disgusting, scheming monster."

She bites him. He should have seen that coming. He sits back with a hiss only to have her rear up and catch him in the groin. With a grunt, he's knocked off balance, and she tries to take up his weapon for herself. The black magic of it sears her immediately, the sizzle audible, and she cries out. Staggering, she lets it topple back into the grass while she looks at her reddened palm.

Zanth snatches his sword and is up again, swinging down and pressing forward, making her jump back to avoid his brutish stabs. The only sounds are the crickets, the short, rushed breaths they take, and Zanth's blade crackling its dangerous haze through the air.

"My queen only has one goal," she growls. "To destroy you!"

"Yes." He grimaces. "She's made that point quite clear."

He draws two fingers up the flat of his blade and thrusts them toward her. A mist of crimson heat plumes out, the sword's aura extending, but Reyanne drops to the dirt and rolls, finally giving him an attack spell that works. The white grass threads up and around his legs like choking vines, bringing him to his knees with a heavy *thwump* before more starts growing from the ground, latching higher and strangling his hips while she skirts to an unacceptable distance. Slamming his fist down, the grass curls in on itself, burned and brown, aging to nothingness at Zanth's touch, the blackest magic there is. He could make this white witch a withering husk if only he could touch her.

She draws the toe of her boot across the land, making it rumble and crack, bringing him down and caving him in. Zanth's having none of it.

"Pe'kat quinara Tethka!" he spits, dragging Reyanne to follow him under. The earth swallows them both into a dark cavern that lies beneath the surface, an earthen blackness blocking everything from view.

"Lunat!" Reyanne yells, starbursts of light illuminating the stalagmites and stalactites that will prove her dexterity a true advantage. Everything is flickering in chiaroscuro, which is disorienting at the best of times, never mind when he's half blind. A small underground stream makes the air reek of moisture as well, putting Zanth's fire magic at a disadvantage.

Damnit, he silently curses.

She just gives him a cocky look, eyebrows up and smirking. Her fingers crook as she rakes her hand in an upward swipe, calling the water to the air and whistling a tell-tale warble through her teeth, making the droplets turn to ice and shoot forward like pellets. One catches Zanth in the meat of the thigh, but a quick barrier thrown up turns the rest back in her direction. No matter her dodging, she can't move fast enough. One pummels through her upper arm, leaving a wavering line of blood in its wake. They're even now, wound-for-wound.

"I like when you fight me." Zanth grins. "It makes it worth killing you."

She sneers at the gash across her skin. Swiping the blood off, she draws a red line down her right temple, and immediately Zanth's good eye burns.

Gasping, his hand flies up to cover it. "Bitch!"

Nice to know you'll use black magic when it suits you, he thrusts into her mind.

He only feels her smug satisfaction, her thoughts tumbling over spell after spell, intentionally trying to confuse him. Closing his mind, Zanth opens his ears instead and hears her kick off the stones on the ground, coming at him with God knows what in store.

"Kah-hana!" he shouts, locking everything out save sound, and she ricochets off his invisible barrier with a screech as lightning courses through her body.

"Etatsa," he hisses, drawing a rune symbol over his good eye, dispelling her magic and letting himself see once more.

Reyanne is lying at an odd angle, staring at him with her mouth gaping. He can barely see anything but her face in the tangle of spiked stalagmites around them, so he takes two steps to the side, her eyes following him. Three steps and he sees her boot twitching. Four and he can see her dirty knees trembling under ripped pants. Five and he sees something he'll never unsee.

She's impaled.

Zanth's vision is still foggy, but he takes in what protrudes through the soft center of her, blood seeping through her white clothes and trailing up the rock surface that's destroyed her.

There's no surviving this. She tries to make a healing symbol in the air, but can't lift her hand properly, her muscles weak from the electric shock his barrier caused. The bolt of energy must have knocked her back, skewering her in the process. Zanth shakes his head, mouth agape. Somewhere deep inside, he knows this isn't what he wanted.

It doesn't matter. It's too late.

"Shh," he says, kneeling beside her, tucking an errant strand of hair behind her ear as red trickles from her nose and the corner of her mouth. "Bear with it, princess. It will be over soon."

She gags and gurgles, her insides fluttering in panic, but there's nothing for it. Her eyes are glassy and in a constant state of surprise as her chest hitches over and over. He finds he wants to share in her pain, but for once, her sensations are mute. Their bond has been broken. He's been connected to her mind all this time yet there are so many things he's never said—will never get the chance to say—but there's one thing he must finally confess.

"I could have loved you," he tells her softly.

Her lips tick up at the corners as her eyes begin to close.

Perhaps in another life, she whispers into his mind, and Zanth knows those are the last words she'll ever say. It leaves him lightheaded. Reeling. He may be sick.

A part of Zanth dies with her. The part that dreamed. The part that hoped for more. The part that nearly kissed her not ten minutes earlier.

Suddenly, the world seems to have lost its color.

More than anything, this cements him in the darkness. Fury boils as he stares at her, wishing for lives he cannot live.

Longing for love he cannot have. Lamenting futures that have burned away in one fell swoop, and by his own design. It's with this new, writhing hate that Zanth will destroy the vestiges of the Separatists. There are none who will escape his wrath now…

…for if not her, then no one.

You, dear reader, have earned a <u>BAD ENDING</u>!

Remember, there are 17 possible endings, and this is just one. If you've found all eight Zanthrand endings, start back at the beginning, and choose Reyanne's path. Many diverging stories await you!

Good luck, dear reader!

CHAPTER 29

Zanth reaches in fast, latching onto the back of her neck just like he did in their dream. Her mouth drops open as he pulls her in, lips parting and his one eye gazing at her reaction.

It's a bad one.

Her face twists and she bucks away, putting him at a distance.

"How did you know to do that?" she asks through gritted teeth.

He can't come up with a response quick enough, so she looks inside him—a rare occurrence—and finds exactly what she's searching for.

"You invaded my dream," she accuses.

For some reason, the derisive tone in her voice upsets him more than angers him. He defends himself without thinking. "You were *gone*, Reyanne! For all these years you've been in my mind, you were suddenly a void in our bond!"

"I've taken draughts before!"

"But never for so long!"

She sneers. "I had no idea what you'd do to me today. But

of all the things I'd considered, it was not this! I don't want this!"

Zanth's pride stings, and his anger returns. "Don't you, though? Isn't that what I saw in your mind? Remember, *princess*, I can tell when you're lying."

Her hands ball into fists. "Get out of my head."

"You don't realize how deep this goes." Though he's beginning to. "I feel like we've always been connected to each other, even before you stitched our minds. Who are you to say it's not the will of the cosmos?"

"It's only the will of a sick, disgusting man who wishes to dominate anything and everything he sees. Including me!"

Zanth's good eye couldn't narrow farther if it tried.

DEAR READER,
Does Zanth get rough? Turn to page 190 (chapter 30)
Or does he back off? Turn to page 203 (chapter 31)

CHAPTER 30

Rearing forward, Zanth grabs her wrist and pulls her close, overpowering her in the way only he can. "If you won't admit that you feel this, I'll force you to. If I give it, you will take every last drop."

He wraps around with both arms, clutching her waist and the curve of her neck even as she shoves at him. It doesn't matter. Still, something within him keeps his mouth soft as he kisses her. Plush. When she tries to bite, he nuzzles under her neck instead, running his lips over her pulse and suckling her skin. She makes noises then—perfect, high gasps of shock and pleasure—but the feeling of her through their bond is one of pure panic.

He may be a monster, but there are limits. He shakes his head in the crook of her neck before releasing her, backing up and looking away at the stunted grass.

What am I doing? he wonders, uncaring if she hears him or not. *It wasn't supposed to be this way.*

But he doesn't know how it was supposed to be anymore.

Looking up, she's staring at him with wide eyes, taking him in toes to crown. Her hand is clasped over where he'd tried to seduce her, covering the sensitive arch of her neck like it's been wounded. "You didn't do that in my dream."

His gaze burns. "But I wanted to." Another truth. "I think I'm going crazy."

Fight gone out of her, she murmurs, "I must be, too…"

"For trusting me?" he asks, his tone derisive. "For coming here?"

"For dreaming about you in the first place." Putting her hands over her face, she shields herself from his regard. "Why did I dream about you, Zan?"

He has no answers. None that make sense. "Do you want me, Reyanne? In your most secret of hearts, do y—"

"Don't say it," she whispers through her fingertips, shaking her head.

Zanth takes a deep breath in through his nose and holds it, counting in slow ticks to keep his composure. "You tied us together—"

"Stop," she tries.

"You fight me yet refuse to destroy me."

"Zan, please…"

"I think that your dreams are more honest than you are."

She finally looks at him.

"And here I stand, bearing my belly to you, offering to let you have what you long for. You want my touch? My heart? My loyalty? Ask me for it, princess. Ask me and I'll give you anything."

The look in her eyes changes into something more intense. Heated. She flicks her gaze to his lips once more.

"Do you need me to beg?" He swallows thickly. "Because I will."

And with that, she's the one who steps forward this time. With quick strides, she closes the distance in seconds and launches herself into his arms, forcing him to catch her under the curve of her rear as she grips the sides of his face, the palm of one hand pressing into the scar she gave him. His back arches to counter her weight as she stares into him.

"Gods help me," she whispers.

Then she kisses him.

She's untrained, as she should be. Zanth knows quite well that she's never taken a man to her bed. But she's a woman of war, and encampments are full of people who would comfort each other after a hard day's battle in the only way they knew how. Oh, how he'd felt her blush and look away when she would happen upon a couple lost in pleasure. He had smiled from afar, delighting in her embarrassment…

Yet that's not what his woman feels now. She feels possessive. She feels needy, greedy, and half out of her mind.

He'll join her in that.

As she kisses him in rough presses, he tries to soften her attack with nudges and tiny licks at the seam of her mouth. Reyanne is a quick study, and soon Zanth's mind is euphoric with the attention she's blessing him with. The taste of her is addictive, and he knows he'll never be the same.

Sinking to his knees, he takes her down to the white ground beneath them, still daytime-warm even as the moon sits high. Her eyes are colorless in the semi-dark, but it takes nothing away from her beauty. She's always been stunning, even on the battlefield. Flecked with blood and slick with sweat, she is his warrior goddess.

She straddles his lap, and he can feel his erection pulse, riding against where her body is the warmest and causing an erotic thrill to run up his belly and spine in tandem. She pulls back with a sharp intake of breath, her irises searching his.

"What was that?" she asks.

Well, that's interesting.

He widens his hand on the small of her back and tilts his hips up, getting that same thrill, only to watch her eyes flutter closed.

"You feel me," he says in awe. It only makes sense. They feel one another's pain; why wouldn't they feel each other's pleasure? "Let's experiment, shall we?"

He slides his thumbs under the hem of her shirt and lifts his eyebrows, amused when she nods faster than anything. Should the sun shine at this moment, Zanth knows she would be blushing again, afraid but not at the same time.

Trust.

How strange to find it here of all places.

He tugs her clothing up, and she lifts her arms willingly. He takes her breast band with it, leaving her bare to the moonlight. Her breasts are smaller than he'd thought. Tiny little peaks with dark tips.

Having caught the descriptors from his mind, her mood sinks, and she moves to cover herself. He catches her arms and holds them wide. "Don't you dare." With that, he leans forward, nearly taking the whole of her into his mouth with new kinds of kisses. Her nipple hardens immediately as she squeaks a shocked noise. It's he who feels *her* pleasure this time, the corresponding spot on his chest tingling and hardening. He'd never known what this felt like.

Skimming his lips over to her other breast, he does it again. It's like he's seducing himself and using her body to do it. When he drags his teeth over her pebbled peaks, her voice drops to something lower. Pulling back, he blows cool air over her skin, and she twitches, making him even harder. Kissing up her neck, leaving warm wet circles, he tastes the underside of her jaw and beneath her ear. His voice is low to the point of growling as he says, "I want you naked beneath me, princess."

Her head tips back, offering her throat by instinct, and ohh, wouldn't it be so nice to claim her. Bite her. Leave his mark so she'll remember this moment forever.

He gives her sinful whispers, feeling his own skin prickle

at his words. "I want to cover you with my body. I want to put myself inside you. I want to pleasure you until your mind melts, little one. Until you're screaming my name. Do you know what that will do to me?"

He's willing to bet he'll come when she does. Or vice versa.

How miraculous that would be.

He wraps his hands around her shoulders and pulls down, riding her over him and breathing through the sweet sensation. "I'll take every inch of you, my Reyanne."

"Yours?" she asks, her voice a whisper.

"You were always mine. You just didn't know it yet."

Neither did he, but he knows now. It's an undeniable truth.

He leans her backward onto the soft, silken white grass, taking in the sight of her before stripping his own garb in short order.

He'd worn too much. It takes too long. Yet it's worth every minute as he sees her stare at him, sitting up on her elbows with lust in her eyes, appreciating every new inch of skin he reveals. Being strong has always been something he prided himself in, and he finds himself preening under her regard, flexing his shoulders purposefully as he undoes his belt.

In a quick motion, he loops it behind her neck and uses it like reins, pulling her up as he drags himself down, taking her mouth and doing his best to own her desire. He holds her steady this way, refusing to let her come up for air until he feels her swoon.

Leaning back, he flings his belt far and away to give space for other things. She's panting, not even bothering to watch the leather go as he undoes his clothes. All innocence, she spreads her legs wide to give way for him to remove his trousers, not knowing when she's truly offering in that moment. He takes the opportunity to dive down and lick a stripe against the cloth covering her sex. She squeaks and he smiles against her, feeling her surprise and burning interest within his own body.

Taking in the scent of her, he whispers into her mind. *Curious about this, are we?*

Shut up and take my clothes off, is what comes back, making him chuckle.

"As my lady wishes."

She's naked in mere moments, their clothes piled together like the lovers Zanth and Reyanne are about to become. He thinks about his rooms in his Dominion citadel. The large, lonely bed chambers. The bathtub made for two. The dining set with four chairs—a wish he'd never thought would come true; yet, in this moment, all things are possible as he runs the head of himself in circles against her entrance.

She's wet and soft for him, nearly dripping down his length as he grips himself in his hand, promising her silently that he'll go slow. In truth, he has no desire to. He just wants to impale her and win this new battle. He is courting her body as he runs his chest along hers, pressing their foreheads together as he takes kiss after kiss. He's breathing in her exhales and giving her his own, feeling lightheaded as he nudges in and in, millimeters at a time.

It stings.

It feels good.

He's afraid.

He's ablaze.

He can't pick apart what's him and what's her anymore, so he just advances on her center, easing in. Her fingernails dig into his biceps and the pleasure-pain makes her mouth drop wide. He's going to drown her in his tongue. She's going to swallow him above and below all at once.

It's that thought that sends him home, her slick sheath

grabbing him like a hot vise as he feels every inch of her internal softness.

"Gods, princess."

She likes that. He can tell. There's more she likes, too.

"You feel so good. Can you feel what this is like for me?"

"Y-yes," she manages.

He pulls his hips back slightly only to split her open again with a low moan. "Say my name."

And she does.

He arches his back, keeping his rhythm shallow and letting her build from pain to pleasure. It's working, slowly but surely. His speed increases, whimpering in sync with her, marveling as her hot wetness travels, making the cool air of the night caress his length before he pushes back into her awaiting heat. It's been a long time since he's felt this. Far too long.

"Reyanne…I…"

Her hand snakes up and fists in his hair, pulling his head back and making him buck in a hard thrust. With a seductive gasp, she hooks her heels around his hips and clenches, pulling him in deeper. Her body is sucking him in, refusing to let him leave, and his abdomen is tensing in that tell-tale sign of oncoming release.

I have to pull back, he tells her.

But she only holds him tighter. Every time he tries to remove himself, he is refused, and her need is blocking out his rational mind.

Reyanne, please.

But her fist tugs harder, and it feels so perfect it distracts him completely. Her pleasure is his. Her sheath is a phantom area within him that begs to be filled. And *filled.* And *fucking filled.*

Giving up and giving in, he pounds into her, hooking a hand under her knee and hiking her leg high. Forget moans, she's screaming his name in guttural cries and he's dying. He's inside her, around himself, grabbing at his body, splitting her apart, and he can't, he can't, he *can't.*

He bursts inside her with a cry, and she follows him over the edge, clamping down in shuddering waves and milking him for all he's worth as he continues to make love to her—because, make no mistake, in this moment, even if never again, they are in love. They belong to each other. They are everything they need in this world.

He collapses atop her and feels the heavy rise and fall of her chest as she pants, a sheen of sweat dappling her body. He's still inside her, never wanting to leave, not wanting the moment to break apart.

Yet it does.

Suddenly, shame is all she feels. And sorrow. He watches as her eyes fill with tears that cascade like streams. A thought runs circles in her mind.

What have I done?

Zanth is filled with regret. Hers, not his. What he feels is pain. This could have been the moment to end all their loneliness and suffering. A chance to become something more together. But no. She's just another disappointment in a lifetime of them, and Zanth is tired of playing her game.

Pulling back, he leaves her cold. Picking up her white clothes, he uses them to wipe himself, removing the scarlet of her maidenhead and all signs of his passion before throwing it at her. Let her people see her marked with his seed and know *exactly* what she's done.

She cringes when it hits her, immediately sitting up and hunching over herself as he continues to toss pale garb her way, slinging on his own dark blue robes with little preamble. Letting out a high-pitched whistle, he calls Stilte, and the beautiful black mare lands gracefully by his side.

"Zan, say something."

He doesn't bother looking at her. "You disgust me."

He mounts his steed and pats her neck. The only female obedient to him out of love lifts her body on perfect wings, and the wind travels through his hair—messy because of that abhorrent white witch. His body still feels the aftermath of ecstasy, but he lets his hurt overtake it.

He hates her, and hates her, and *hates her.*

Even though she doesn't echo that feeling back at him. All he senses from her is sadness.

Good.

* * *

They had ignored each other for days…until General Alec Schezain launched his new weapon. It was all the Separatists could do to try and contain it. An army of trebuchets launched boulders covered in burning oil, but that wasn't all. The oil was noxious after it had burned for a few minutes, and at the site of their calamity, those who were not crushed or incinerated breathed in its colorless essence and died, foaming at the mouth. It was brutal. It was a massacre. Schezain always was a sadist.

It was more damage than Zanth wanted to do to those who would eventually become his citizens, but demoralizing them was a key part of Zanth's strategy. Only then did the white witch come back, strumming on their bond with fury, trying to get into his head. Zanth did his best to burn her with searing scolds in his mind.

Weeks passed like that. Then a month. Then two. Then she started trying to invade his dreams, so he slept less and less, refusing her as much as he was able. At first, her mental touches—though filled with vitriol—were easy to fend off.

But soon her energy became more frantic, panicked, until she outright *slammed* herself into his mind.

Lying in his bed toward the early dawn, he hears her ask: *What do I do?*

Die a slow and horrible death, he replies.

She opens his mind's eye within her, and Zanth sees his mother staring Reyanne down, cold cruelty in her eyes.

"Who did this to you?" the queen demands.

Zanth feels the white witch want to sink into the floor.

Queen Jehanne strides in front of Reyanne in nighttime garb, pacing, her hair uncoiffed. Zanth's erstwhile uncle stands beside Reyanne, arms crossed, face drenched with suspicion and disdain.

"I—I don't know how it happened," Reyanne says, though it feels like a lie.

"On the battlefield, perhaps?" Leif Cassian pries. "Did you indulge?" He speaks as if Reyanne were a child, and she tenses. Zanth can feel every clench of it, their mental connection wide open. He should shut her down, but his morbid curiosity wins out.

"My soldiers are just that. My *soldiers,*" she says. "There is a chain of command to be followed. I would never—"

"Then who?" Zanth's mother cuts her off. "One of the other mages?"

"Why does it matter?" Reyanne asks, desperation and fear filling her chest to the point of choking.

"It *matters* because my biggest asset only has months before she's useless. It matters that all my hard work and all the people who have died will have died in vain due to you! Now, tell me who did this!"

Help me, Reyanne begs him, but Zanth still doesn't know what's going on. Her eyes burn and she can't breathe.

Zanth watches Leif Cassian—the man who tried to kill

him as a boy, his first master and mentor—narrow his eyes into slits. "It was the Dark Moon."

And Reyanne lets her tears fall. Zanth sits up in bed, confusion carving stripes in his mind.

"Why the fuss?" Leif sneers. "Upset to be caught or upset to be carrying his spawn in the first place?"

Zanth's blood runs cold. *My what...?* But Reyanne is beyond hearing him at this point. Her eyes must be closed because the vision cuts to blackness.

He hears his mother's soft musing as she says, "That *conversation* he tricked you into..." Sympathy rolls within the sound of Queen Annora Jehanne's voice now. "Oh, Reyanne. Did he take something that didn't belong to him?"

An electric bolt of disgust sizzles through him. It's clear Reyanne doesn't understand, but her vision snaps back open to see his mother's face drenched in sympathy.

"He did, didn't he?"

TELL HER NO! Zanth screams without sound, but Reyanne doesn't understand, too young and inexperienced for their own good.

"He...he hurt me," is what falls from that traitorous witch's mouth.

Oh, you bitch. You little bitch.

But you did, she sends back. *You hurt my feelings.*

THAT'S NOT WHAT SHE'S ASKING! Zanth's anger boils over and he thrusts his hand sideways, magically shoving everything beside his bed to a distance and shattering ceramic pieces on the floor. Wash basins, decanters, even the oaken tables splinter.

"I'm so sorry, Reyanne," his mother says. "I'm sorry to have doubted your honor. It's settled, then. We'll take it out of you."

Zanth rears up, wanting to destroy. "No!" comes from his and Reyanne's mouths simultaneously.

"It's mine!" she continues. "It's my hope for the future!"

What do you know of hope? Zanth seethes.

His uncle tsks in a way that makes Zanth's blood boil. "My dear, one has to wonder why would you want the child of the man who raped you."

Zanth feels Reyanne's heart drop and her breath leave her.

TELL THEM I DIDN'T! I'M A MAN OF WAR, BUT I HAVE LIMITS! GIVE ME MY DIGNITY!

At the cost of my own? she replies, hurt and anger and maliciousness stabbing at him.

"If you're as righteous as you say, you should care about the truth," Zanth spits aloud, knowing she hears every word.

He feels Reyanne think about turning into a ball of light to escape, but she doesn't know what it will do to the baby. Zanth's baby. *Their* baby. She thinks about running, but that will only damn her, and they'll take it from her anyway— either by magic, by medicine, or by force. She thinks about telling her people the truth, but knows it will result in her execution, a fact Zanth had never considered. He hadn't considered much of anything. Only that she needed to be his.

"Rape or not, hate or not, enemy or not, this child is mine," Reyanne says, and Zanth knows that's as a good a defense as he's going to get from her. He hates her with new flavor. New nuance. Intrusive, obsessive thoughts make sickly scars in his soul.

I could hunt you down, white witch. I could steal my regretful lover and my innocent child away. Yet something in him shifts, making him add, *You'd be in no danger. You'd want for nothing.*

Except love, she replies, and Zanth's heart cracks.

Let me stay with the Separatists, she continues. *This war may be over soon. And you may even win.*

Win or lose, if you fight, this war could end you, especially when your magic and body weaken!

Then I'll run from all this, she says, their exchange taking mere moments as Reyanne holds her hands defensively over her lower belly. *I'll leave and never come back.*

If you're not with them, you're with me, he says.

I'm with no one but myself.

It's too late for that, now.

Zan, please.

Hearing her say his name in such a plaintive matter moves him, somehow. His rage is a razor's edge, yet tipping into mercy—the mercy she's shown him. But, then again, he is who he is. Why should he change it now for this treacherous witch?

Dear reader,

Does Zanth vow to hunt her down? Turn to page 208 (chapter 32)

Or does he agree to watch them from afar? Turn to page 210 (chapter 33)

CHAPTER 31

He backs away slowly, every step almost painful. A deep shame burns him, and she feels it. "I'm no stranger to rejection, white witch, but there are very few who insult me and live."

He's trying to disguise his hurt as something else, something angry and familiar, but his heartache wins out, even so. He's been frantically searching for her through their bond for days, but she doesn't feel this urgency. Perhaps she never will. "I was a fool to come."

Reyanne drops her chin, his heartache softening her. She blinks back tears, rubbing at her eyes. "This isn't a rejection of you, but what you stand for. Things could be so much different if—"

"If I were a different man. A man with my power, my face and nothing else."

She tries to speak, but comes up with nothing, damning him all the worse. He's crushed. He can barely breathe for the lump in his throat.

No one ever wants me. Not myself, not my family, and not even my soulmate.

"That's not what we are," she says aloud.

"Isn't it? When you're gone, I need you. When you could kill me, you don't. Even when my whole world revolves around destroying you, I can't bring myself to do it! It's like the future has been set before me, and every path that's worth anything leads to you!"

A tear falls over her cheek. "You're trying to kill everyone that matters to me. You're trying to destroy what I've helped build."

"And aren't you doing the exact same?"

Reyanne's lower lip quivers. Cradling herself with her arms, she shakes her head slightly. "I wish I could run away. I wish for more than just an end to the war; I want to pretend I had no part in it. I want to pretend you didn't either." Her face crumbles. "I want to hide in a hole in the ground where it's safe and just live a life with no one!"

"Except me?" he tries.

Bursting into tears, she says, "I'm so lonely."

And he knows. Zanth echoes that feeling back, and their emotions feed each other, one to the next, until suddenly she's crying in his arms, and he doesn't even know how she got there.

"I'm tired..." he murmurs into her hair. "I don't want to do this anymore."

"We have to. This goes beyond us."

"But does it need to?"

She blinks up at him.

"We are not the entire world, Reyanne. There are other places. Over the mountains, across the seas." He pulls her in closer, tucking her under his chin and stroking his fingers through her earth-toned hair, the motion as comforting to him as it is to her. "With our skill, we could live alone. We could fend for ourselves, feed ourselves, build a home for ourselves—"

"Build a family together."

She says it quietly, but it's as loud as a thunderclap. She's almost ashamed of herself, trying to pull away, but he only holds her tighter.

"And we'll love them," he says. "We'll care for them from the moment they're born until the moment we die."

"If we leave here, what happens?"

Zanth curls over, burying his face in the crook of her neck. "It doesn't matter. Having you here like this, I feel more complete than I have my entire life. If you let go of me now, I'll break. I'll shatter. I'll go mad. Please..." he begs.

She nuzzles closer. "I don't know what to do."

He pulls back and presses a gentle kiss to her trembling lips. He whispers over her mouth, "Yes you do." His nose caresses hers, his thumbs running under her jaw. "Stay with me."

She doesn't say yes, not with words, but his white witch reaches around, lacing her fingers together behind his neck and pulling him into another kiss.

"We're abandoning them," she says, but Zanth is lost in the scent of her. The feeling of her. The words spoken may as well have been the breeze.

"Stay," he repeats. "Make me a family. Let me love you from today until the last day."

He feels the exact moment she gives in, and it's ecstasy. His kisses grow deeper until he is drowning in her. She is every last drop of moonlight and every star in the sky.

Soon, he will fly his bride to lands unknown. They will be assumed dead, and the war will go on without them, but he will be free. Free from the fear of constant betrayal, for he can read his white witch's mind. Free from the hate in his heart, for all those he despises will be too far away to catch his thoughts. Free from loneliness, for the woman he's longed for will be by his side, held tight against him, wrapped around him, giving him all she is. It's worth letting go of whatever has come before, for there is everything else to gain.

"Let's run away," she says, the sweetest words Zanth has ever heard.

"Thank you, princess."

And, just like that, his future is unwritten. His path forward unclear. His fate his own.

It's the most wonderful feeling he's ever known.

You, dear reader, have earned a <u>HAPPY ENDING</u>!

One of two in the Zanth track! Good job, you!

Remember, there are 17 possible endings, and this is just one. If you've found all eight Zanthrand endings, start back at the beginning, and choose Reyanne's path. Many diverging stories await you!

Good luck, dear reader!

CHAPTER 32

*R*un, *then, Reyanne. But don't think I won't catch you.*

With that, Zanth cuts their connection again, his heart in his throat.

He is going to have a child.

His eyes cast in the direction of his small dining room, the physical manifestation of his heart's fondest wish. In just a few moments, Zanth's long-held hope for a family has now become a tangible thing. A real possibility instead of a foolish dream.

If Reyanne won't stay with him, he'll keep the child at least. Perhaps then there would then be someone in this world who would love him. Someone innocent and untainted. He can be a good father; he knows it. He just has to keep Reyanne safe until then. Once the child is weaned, the white witch can go free. Though he must admit, he can't imagine letting her go.

He'd have to take away her magic, then—but how to do it without truly hurting her? Mages usually have their tongues cut out and the first two fingers removed from each of their hands to keep them from doing spells, but he couldn't bear to do that to her. Killing her would be swift, but leaving her to suffer, forever stunted, is another thing entirely. If he does have mercy, it's in that alone.

Standing, he dresses quickly, slinging his robes over his shoulders. No longer in midnight blue, he dresses in purest black, for there's no one to deceive anymore. Zanth takes hold of his darkness, his cruelty, and strides into his throne room, servants awaiting his beck and call.

"Build a nursery adjacent to my chambers. Make two additional rooms, besides. They all must be lockable with the most intricate, magic-resistant material possible. Line the whole place with it. I need to trap a powerful sorceress within my walls. Make it comfortable, colorful, beautiful, but complete it as quickly as possible. Day or night, it matters not. I will sleep elsewhere."

And what can his people do but agree?

In the meantime, he needs to find a way to capture his reluctant woman. This is going to be a new kind of battle, but one he is absolutely willing to fight. After all, the prize is making his dreams come true.

If not in one way, then in another…

You, dear reader, have earned an <u>OPEN</u> <u>ENDING</u>!

Remember, there are 17 possible endings, and this is just one. If you've found all eight Zanthrand endings, start back at the beginning, and choose Reyanne's path. Many diverging stories await you!

Good luck, dear reader!

CHAPTER 33

*R*un, *then, Reyanne.*

And with that, Zanth retreats from his side of the bond.

* * *

Ergol launches from Zanth's arm, taking his secret message to the Separatists' stronghold. Will Reyanne be watched closely now? If so, this plan may fail on two fronts. One, he may expose that he and Reyanne are working together, and two, he may reveal his long-hidden spy. Either way, he's losing the asset he has deeply rooted within his enemy's ranks. Lilah Tai.

She has sat in the Separatists leadership as a trusted healer and tactician, feeding the Dominion all sorts of delicious intelligence over the last few years. Zanth keeps Lilah's sister hostage, making the girl write just enough letters to keep his spy motivated. The girl is locked up tight, but not without a key, and that key is Lilah's servitude. Once this war was over with the Dominion as the victor, Lilah was to earn her sister's freedom and a lifetime of wealth. Now, though, Zanth is willing to release Lilah's sister much sooner, so long as his spy succeeds in her new task: smuggling Reyanne and his unborn babe from those who would do them harm…and as fast as possible.

Lilah hates Zanth, but his leverage on her can't be over-stated. She'll do anything he tells her to. He can only wonder how Reyanne will react when she learns her colleague has been working for the Dominion all this time, and how Lilah will take it when she realizes that the white witch and the man she so loathes are soul-bound.

Zanth will have to leave himself open to Reyanne's emotions. He's darkly interested in how that conversation will play out.

* * *

Their bond rips the air, the portal flinging them into the same space for the first time in a long while. It's been months now, and neither Zanth nor Reyanne have deigned to speak to one another—not even when the mirror gate has opened —yet here and now, Zanth finds himself torn from the comfort of his chambers and dumped into a field under a thin tent, just barely staving off the chill.

He sits up, wrapping his arms around his shoulders as his skin turns to goose flesh under his thin sleeping clothes. Instead of a warm bed coated with soft furs, he's forced to face winter approaching, the crisp cold dusting the air with its scent.

Looking at Reyanne, he finds her lying under a blanket,

thick and knit. In the dark, they stare at each other, not knowing what to do. They could attack each other. Scream at each other. Ignore each other. Or…

He mouths the word, "Lilah?" with his eyebrows up and Reyanne tics her jaw toward a tent wall.

Next one over, she says.

He nods, knowing that speaking aloud is now out of the question.

Your eye… she says, tapping her cheek.

He had almost forgotten. *I healed it.*

It glows. Why? Can it actually see?

And more. He nods sharply, unwilling to disclose the nature of the new power of sight he'd given himself. His gaze flicks to her midsection, well hidden, but his new eye can see the aura of warmth inside her anyway. It looks golden and bright. His heart pangs, but he bites the inside of his cheek, unsure of what to say. Instead, he focuses on ignoring the cold.

Her next words are, *Have you won the war?*

He eyes her. *Don't you know?*

She shrugs under her blankets, frowning in a way that's almost adorable. *We're on the run. We don't talk to anyone if it's not to buy supplies.*

I have, he admits. *The battles are over, and the integration has begun. My offer is open, Reyanne. Come to my castle and I'll give you everything you need. When the snow falls, you don't want to have a newborn in your arms as you fight for dirty spaces at cheap inns.*

She sighs, scrubbing her eyes. Zanth knows Lilah has had this conversation with Reyanne many times. It's in her weekly reports. Zanth may not be on good speaking terms with the mother of his child, but that doesn't mean he's not keeping a close eye. Deciding not to press the issue, he hunches closer into himself, shivering. With another heavy sigh, Reyanne flips her covers open to offer him a space beside her.

At first, he can't move. He's staring at the curve of her belly. His new eye lets him see clearly even in the night, and looking at her like this is enough to make him weak. His lip trembles at the round reality of her, of what they've made.

"Zan," she whispers so quietly, it's almost inaudible. Tucking her chin down, she indicates beside her again. *Hurry. It's cold.*

He swallows roughly and moves to lie beside her, stiff as she swoops the warm blanket over them both. Without warning, she tucks a leg over his hips and snuggles in. His eyes couldn't fly wider if they tried.

Shh, she silently scolds. *It's more comfortable this way. You'd know what this ball of baby feels like if you weren't blocking your side of the bond.*

And aren't you doing the same?

Don't fight. I'm too tired. She huffs, digging her nose into his shoulder as her fist yanks the blanket higher up his chest.

He doesn't know what to do with himself. Tense, Zanth's body is a rock as he feels her newfound softness pressing against him. No longer rail thin, her breasts are filling out, and her belly...

Yes, my belly, she gripes. *And it's only going to get bigger, thank you very much.*

A smile tugs at his lips. *Between the two of us, princess, I'm the only one who even made an attempt to stop this very scenario.*

And she bites him, once, on the shoulder. It's not hard—to get a point across more than anything else—but it startles him into a hiss. Her hand clamps over his mouth in short order as she looks over to the tent wall, listening.

I think Lilah's asleep, Reyanne says.

Well, thank the Gods for that.

He settles in a bit more, unsure of what to do with his

hands. The weight of Reyanne's touch is pleasant, warming the little spaces in his heart while their connection soothes a wound he'd carved into his mind by slicing her out of it. From the look in her eyes, it seems his white witch is feeling the same. There is a healing happening right now, of one kind or another. Maybe all kinds.

Her hair is greasy, tied back in braided pleats. She smells of dirty clothes and sweat. She—

Bites him again, and he grunts this time.

Not everyone can smell like perfume and lilies, Zanthrand.

He considers. *And what do I smell like?*

She grumps. *Perfume and lilies.*

He grins at that.

Would you like to touch it? Reyanne asks, and Zanth's heart throbs. He's never ached for anything the way he has for this.

Letting her take control, she lifts his hand and places it on the swell of their child. There are flutters and pushes against his palm as it moves.

Suddenly, a flash whites out Zanth's mind, his new eye dipping him into an all-encompassing vision, an unexpected experience elevated beyond any divination he's ever had before. Locked in his reverie, sparkling dew has left a heady scent on the air, and Zanth can feel cool grass on his bare feet. Before him is the tinkling bell of a child's laughter. Midnight hair, just like his, and eyes of hazel greet him with a smile. This is what their baby will become. Strong. Healthy. Kindness shines bright in the child's eyes as it plays in the summertime warmth. Happiness and contentment surround this vision, wrapping it in softness and love.

He's going to cry.

Reyanne is already crying. *It knows daddy is here.*

She, Zanth corrects. *She knows daddy is here.*

Reyanne sniffles but doesn't argue.

Do you regret it? he asks.

Every day. But I wouldn't take it back. I want to meet our baby.

And then, Zanth's tears do fall. He spreads his fingers wider, trying to touch as much of Reyanne's rounded tummy as he can. He might never be able to hold his child in the flesh, but he can hold her this way, right now. His heart has bloomed a gaping chasm meant to be filled with this new, little soul, but as long as she's alive, that's what truly matters. He's made something to last beyond him. Even if someday, his daughter becomes yet another enemy set to destroy him, he has no regrets—save one.

"I wish I could be in her life," Zanth whispers.

Reyanne sniffles. "I wish, too."

And, at that, their connection fades, leaving Zanth alone in his room once more.

You, dear reader, have earned an <u>OPEN ENDING</u>!

Remember, there are 17 possible endings, and this is just one. If you've found all eight Zanthrand endings, start back at the beginning, and choose Reyanne's path. Many diverging stories await you!

Good luck, dear reader!

For a follow up to this chapter, check out the author's blog at: https://nixcomix.com/blog

ABOUT THE AUTHOR

From the Boston area, Nichol is a fan of all things art. Known for her weirdness and general snarkasm, Nichol works to engage her audience in several mediums. Many stick to one favorite genre, but she can't seem to make up her mind. You will see her dipping into everything from graphic horror, graphic novels, to graphic romance. Trust the descriptions, mind the tags and just know that, if you like her writing, you're in for a good ride.

Visit her at nixcomix.com to read exclusive short stories, see more about what books are coming out next, watch author interviews and more.

Find her on social media:
Twitter / TikTok / YouTube – **Nixcomix**
Tumblr / Instagram – **Nixcomix1**

Prepare to be surprised

THE RETELLING OF FAIRY TALES is a reimagining of some of our most beloved childhood stories for an adult audience, adding twists and turns that bring them into fantasy worlds, modern day settings, alien planets, and may even take the point of view of the villain.

Fully illustrated, this collection will make you laugh, pull your heartstrings, and let you fall in love. Come with us and enjoy the call of destiny, the sizzle of romance, the ache of tragedy, and the timelessness of magic, all wrapped together in this one unforgettable collection of short stories.

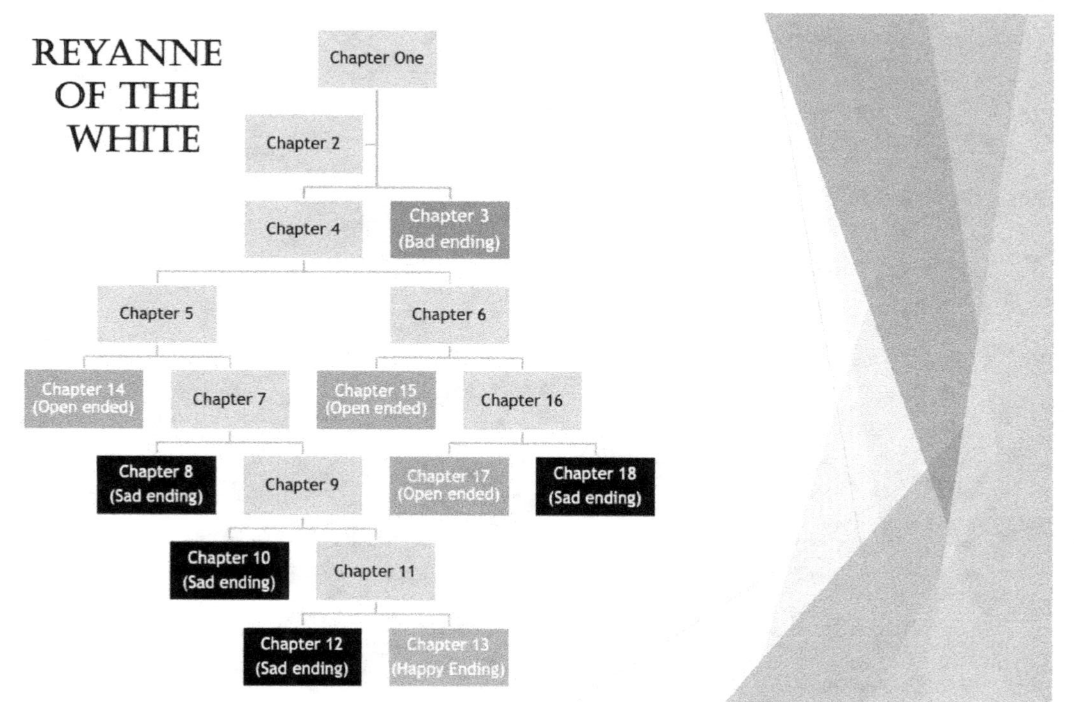

REYANNE OF THE WHITE
Chapter One
Chapter 2
Chapter 4
Chapter 3 (Bad ending)
Chapter 5
Chapter 6
Chapter 14 (Open ended)
Chapter 7
Chapter 15 (Open ended)
Chapter 16
Chapter 8 (Sad ending)
Chapter 9
Chapter 17 (Open ended)
Chapter 18 (Sad ending)
Chapter 10 (Sad ending)
Chapter 11
Chapter 12 (Sad ending)
Chapter 13 (Happy Ending)

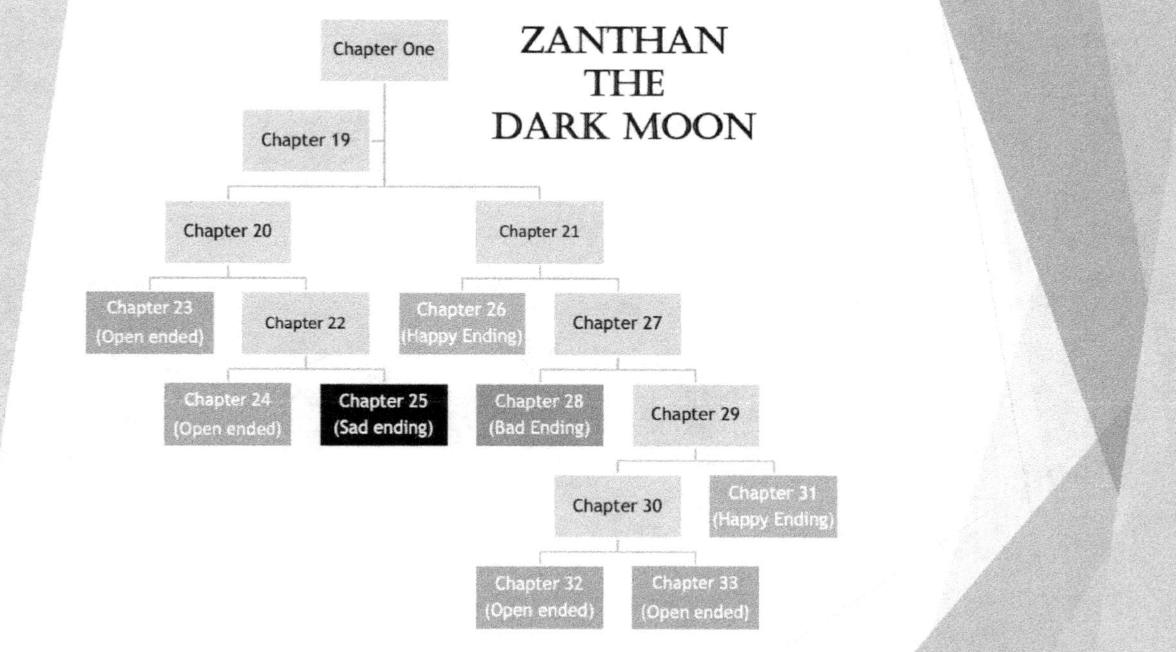

ZANTHAN
THE
DARK MOON
Chapter One
Chapter 19
Chapter 20
Chapter 21
Chapter 23
(Open ended)
Chapter 22
Chapter 26
(Happy Ending)
Chapter 27
Chapter 24
(Open ended)
Chapter 25
(Sad ending)
Chapter 28
(Bad Ending)
Chapter 29
Chapter 30
Chapter 31
(Happy Ending)
Chapter 32
(Open ended)
Chapter 33
(Open ended)

www.ingramcontent.com/pod-product-compliance
Lightning Source LLC
Chambersburg PA
CBHW070506300726
48975CB00007B/2346